What Readers Have Said
About the Viking Quest Books

"I really enjoyed the character Bree and her exciting adventures. I was really amazed with Bree's courage. Even though she was taken from her family and to a different country she knew nothing about, she still had courage . . . Thank you again for such a well-written, exciting book."

—Christoffer, 12, Taiwan

"I just have to say that the Viking Quest books are the best. I love them! I feel myself trusting more in God after these books."

—Alyssa, 15, Colorado

"I like that your characters pray before they hit panic point. And it's encouraging to read books—especially Viking Quest novels—that stress family relationships."

—Ben, Minnesota, age 17

"I wanted to write and tell you how much I enjoyed *Raiders from the Sea,* the first Viking Quest book. I know it says on the back that the book is for ages ten and up. But I, as a 19-year-old, loved it!"

—Rachel, 19, Minnesota

"I just finished the first two books of the Viking Quest series. My mother's family is from Norway and my father's family is Scottish, Irish, and English, so I have a great love of any Celtic or Scandinavian based book. . . . Thank you so much for the work you are doing in making well written, Christian books available to young people."

—Hannah, 14, Missouri

"I just finished reading the three books in the Viking Quest series. I bought them for my 9-year-old son, but couldn't put them down myself! I started reading *Raiders of the Sea* to my boys yesterday (ages 9 and 5). They protested profusely when I told them we had to stop so they could go to bed. When I got up this morning, my 9-year-old son was on the couch reading."

——**Donna Meier,** Connecticut

"I just wanted to let you know your new Viking series is amazing! I've never been into reading, but for some reason or another, your books capture me and I finish them within a couple days! Thank you for what you do."

——**Megan,** 19, Minnesota

"I love your Viking books! When our family reads them aloud together, even our dog listens."

——**Brittany,** 14, Minnesota

"I have ordered the book already from CBD (That is how much I can't wait until February!!!!). I love your books and web site!!!!!"

——**Lyndsey,** 15, Ohio

"We received *The Invisible Friend* today in the mail. I read it all the way through without stopping. Tonight we will start reading these books together as a family. God has blessed you with a wonderful ability to communicate the Gospel through writing."

——**Judy Carter,** Missouri

VIKING ⊛ QUEST book five

the
RAIDER'S
PROMISE

LOIS WALFRID JOHNSON

MOODY PUBLISHERS
CHICAGO

King Olaf Tryggvason, Leif Erikson and his family—father Erik the Red, mother Thjodhild, and brother Thorstein—Bjarni Herjulfsson, Haki and Hekja, Tyrker, Gudrid, Thorir, Thorfinn Karlsefni, and Snorri lived in the time period of this novel. Other characters are fictitious and spring with gratitude for life from the author's imagination. Any resemblance to persons living or dead is coincidental.

All Scripture quotations, unless otherwise indicated, are taken from the *Holy Bible, New International Version®*. NIV®. Copyright © 1973, 1978, 1984 by International Bible Society. Used by permission of Zondervan Publishing House. All rights reserved.

Ps. 77:19; Deut. 31:8; Acts 9:1–9

Published in association with the literary agency of Alive Communications, Inc., 7680 Goddard Street, Suite 200, Colorado Springs, Colorado 80920.

Cover Design: LeVan Fisher Design
Cover and Text Illustrations: Greg Call
Editor: Pam Pugh

ISBN: 0-8024-3116-X
EAN/ISBN-13: 978-0-8024-3116-5

Library of Congress Cataloging-in-Publication Data

Johnson, Lois Walfrid.
    The raider's promise / by Lois Walfrid Johnson.
        p. cm. -- (Viking quest ; bk. 5)
    Summary: Five years after taking Bree and her brother Devin from Ireland to serve as tenth century Viking slaves, Mikkel decides whether to keep his promise to return the pair to their home and restore their freedom.
    ISBN-13: 978-0-8024-3116-5
    1. Vikings—Juvenile fiction. [1. Vikings—Fiction. 2. Slavery—Fiction.
    3. Christian life—Fiction. 4. Norway—History—To 1030—Fiction.
    5. Ireland—History—To 1172—Fiction.] I. Title.

PZ7.J63255Rap 2006
[Fic]—dc22

                                                                 2005021838

We hope you enjoy this book from Moody Publishers. Our goal is to provide high-quality, thought-provoking books and products that connect truth to your real needs and challenges. For more information on other books and products written and produced from a biblical perspective, go to www.moodypublishers.com or write to:

Moody Publishers
820 N. LaSalle Boulevard
Chicago, IL 60610

3 5 7 9 10 8 6 4 2

Printed in the United States of America

To each of you
who has written to me
from America
or from around the world
I dedicate this story
of people
who live with the courage to win.

Thanks for becoming a family of encouragers
and for being my friend through books.

CONTENTS

INTRODUCTION

Beginnings.

Some are scary, but others are fun. The first time you visit a place you've always wanted to see. Meeting someone you want to know. Or being told you're the best in something you've worked hard to accomplish.

Whatever is involved, all beginnings have something in common. You can imagine or expect what it might be like, but you don't really know what will happen until you experience it.

So what was it like to be one of the first Europeans who set foot in a new world? How did they feel, knowing that their choices could make the difference between life and death? If you had been with them would you have needed the courage to win?

Come to think about it, maybe those explorers discovered something we all need. How can you and I live with courage in our everyday lives? And what does it mean to face a life-or-death threat in order to keep a promise?

ONE

LEIF'S DISCOVERY

From high overhead Briana O'Toole heard the cry of a seagull. Pushing aside her reddish-blonde hair, Bree looked up to a flash of wings. In that moment the dangers of the past week seemed far away.

With one swoop the gull landed on the rocky ledge in front of her. Beady eyes upon her, he tipped his head, and shrieked again. A moment later, he lifted his wings and was up and away.

Bree watched him go. Would she ever feel that free again?

Ignoring the uneasiness she felt, Bree watched the gull fly across the water. Early that morning she and others from Leif Erikson's ship had climbed to the top of this island in the great open sea.

As she started back down the steep side, Bree felt the sun on her face and light entered her heart. Then she glanced toward Mikkel.

My enemy, Bree thought out of long habit. But this time she wondered something more. Could he ever become a friend she respected?

Only one year older than Bree, Mikkel had led a raid that carried off rich treasure from the Glendalough Monastery in Ireland. During that raid, his men also captured Bree, her brother, and other Irish from the surrounding countryside.

Nearly four years had passed since that day late in the tenth century, and Mikkel was now eighteen. At a wider place between rocks he turned. "Let's make a new start," he said.

"A new start?" Bree felt the surprise of it. It was his fault that she had become a slave. "Do you really think we can?"

Mikkel looked her straight in the eye. "I'm sure of it." His voice spilled over with confidence. "All we have to do is trust each other."

"Trust." Bree stared at him. Like a storm ready to break, the word hung in the air. How could any trust between them possibly last?

"That's all?" she asked. "Can't you think of something a bit harder?"

Mikkel's grin lit his face. "I'll help you. I'll prove I'm worthy of trust."

Of all the things Mikkel could promise, that was the hardest to imagine. Yet he stood his ground and didn't even blink.

Watching him, Bree wondered how he could feel so sure of himself. Especially now, when they were about to enter a new world. A world where no one, not even Leif Erikson, could know what would happen.

"You'll see," Mikkel promised.

There it was again. The confidence in his voice that he could win. That he could really be trusted to do what he promised. Maybe, just possibly—

If there was anything in the world that Bree wanted, it was being able to believe in Mikkel. If that happened—

For a moment Bree dared to hope. Maybe Mikkel would even take her and her brother Devin home.

Far below, surrounded by the blue waters of the sea, Leif's ship lay anchored in a cove. Some of the men had stayed behind to guard it. As Bree looked down upon them her uneasiness returned.

Leif knows the dangers we face, she tried to tell herself. *Danger to Mikkel and to all of us.* Like the others around her, Bree had learned to value the wise and strong leader of their expedition.

Just then Mikkel spoke again. "Leif's calling."

Leaping between the rocks, Mikkel led the way back

up the steep west side of the island. When they reached the top, Leif stood on a high point, looking across a great expanse of water.

With blond hair and a beard trimmed close to his face, Leif stood taller than most men. Though still a young man, he had earned the respect of everyone who knew him, including the Norwegian king.

"There's something I want you to see." Leif's voice was filled with excitement.

When his crew gathered around him, Bree remembered that as a slave she should stand apart. Instead, she moved forward, wanting to hear every word that Leif said.

But Mikkel left the others behind. Walking out on a rocky ledge, he looked in every direction.

Behind them lay the great expanse of water they had crossed when sailing from Greenland. To their right the blue coast of a rocky wooded land. And ahead of them—

When he turned to Leif, Mikkel's face shone. "A fjord! A waterway leading into the land!"

Leif grinned. "A gateway that will help us explore."

"And good markers!" Mikkel pointed off to his left. Like a gigantic ball of rock, the round head of a cape loomed against the horizon.

To Mikkel's right was another cape. Between that and the round head was a large island with high vertical rock rising from its shore. Beyond lay a long, low point that turned like a beak as it reached into the sea.

"Landmarks no good Viking would miss. And there—" Leif pointed beyond the large island. Though far distant, the rocky ridge of a headland offered another marker.

For a moment Leif turned, looking back to the great open sea over which they had traveled. On the way here they had gone ashore twice as they sailed south. Now in the strong current along that coast an iceberg rose from the water. Though the beginning of July, ice from northern glaciers still offered danger to any ship that passed.

But Leif's face showed only his excitement. "When Thorstein comes—"

Leif and his brother had planned to travel together. While sailing up the coast of Greenland, Leif had learned that Thorstein was delayed.

"He'll follow the same directions from Bjarni that I had," Leif said. "If we're able to use such a good location, he'll find us easily."

As Leif faced the channel again, his voice held the satisfaction of discovery. "It's a gateway, I'm sure of it. A fjord that will open up this new land. Where ships can sail, explorers will come, and settlers, and merchants!"

Once more Leif pointed across the water, this time to a bay between the rocky ridge and the long point of land that extended like a beak into the sea. With his keen eyesight he had seen more than the rest of them.

"That's where we're going," he said. "Ships will not

only be able to see us. Whether friend or enemy, we'll be able to see them."

Friend or enemy. Again Bree felt a warning. Like a bad memory, her dread returned. What about the enemy inside their group? The man who had tried to hurt Mikkel during the trip here?

Starting down between the rocks, Leif led the others. As though he had no thought of the harm that could come to him, Mikkel followed. Son of a Norwegian chieftain, Mikkel often took his rightful place with pride. When the rest of the crew followed, Bree and her brother Devin dropped back.

With all her heart Bree felt excited about the new land they had seen. Yet the possibilities of such a place also made her wonder about her own future. Soon it would be four long years since she had been captured and became a slave. What could she do to change her life?

Partway to the ship, Devin stopped and turned around. Though Bree had inherited their mother's brown eyes and reddish-blonde hair, Devin had the black hair and deep blue eyes of the dark Irish. Like Mikkel, Devin was also eighteen.

As though understanding how Bree felt, Devin offered a brotherly wink. "Remember," he said. "Don't forget who you really are."

In her heart Bree added the words she knew well. *The daughter of a wise and powerful chieftain who loves me very much.*

"Yes, Dev, I know," Bree said aloud.

Even when most angry with Mikkel, she had not blurted out the truth. Afraid that her ransom would go even higher, she had never told Mikkel about her father. Only Bree, Devin, and the Irish captured with them knew the well-kept secret.

Now Bree hugged it to herself. When she entered this new land she would remember. *Though I seem to be a slave, inside I am free. And I won't let anyone take that from me!*

ICEBERG!

Finding one narrow foothold after another, Mikkel followed Leif down the west side of the island. Far below, strong currents flowed around the coast. Leif's ship lay anchored in a rocky cove.

With a high curved bow and stern, the trading vessel had one mast and a large red-and-white sail. From where he stood, Mikkel could see the crew Leif had left behind to stand watch.

Among them were two men, twins who looked exactly alike. Of average height they had broad shoulders, muscular arms, and powerful hands. Though very strong, both moved as quickly and silently as a cat.

One of the men was Mikkel's good friend. The other

was a dangerous enemy. Watching him, Mikkel's hands tightened into fists.

Then Leif stopped. Again he looked across the expanse of water to the new land. "You see it the way I do, don't you?"

Mikkel nodded. "I think so."

Deep inside, Mikkel knew the possibilities of such a place. For years he had thought only about the wealth and fame he could gain through such a trip. When he overcame danger, stories about his mighty deeds would be told in the great halls of the North. He would be honored as one of the great Vikings—master of his own ship and a merchant who crossed the far seas in order to trade valuable goods.

"Those who are first will gain much from the land before us," Mikkel answered. "But now—"

"Yes, now." Leif's gaze was still on the distant shore. "We understand the wealth of this new world. The reward it will bring to us. But we also dare to dream, don't we?"

Feeling the surprise of it, Mikkel agreed. He didn't know Leif's dream, but he knew his own. In his thinking Mikkel had started to go beyond his desire for wealth and fame. *What will this land offer the people who someday live here?*

As he followed Leif onto his merchant ship, Mikkel looked up in surprise. The strong leader was one of the tallest men Mikkel knew. Walking with shoulders back and a long stride, he commanded attention from all who saw him. Yet in that moment Mikkel realized something. Where once he had tipped back his head to look up at Leif, he now stood closer to the leader's height.

Mikkel seldom thought about how much taller he had grown during the three years he lived in Greenland. Today, instead, he felt glad for the strength he had gained and looked forward to using it. *A new world. A new land. A new life?*

He could hardly wait to set foot on the land they had seen from the top of the island.

A large trading vessel, Leif's *knorr* was a wide-body ship with an open hold in the center and small decks at the bow and stern. Approximately sixty-six feet long, it was richly painted above the waterline. Though a *knorr* could carry animals, Leif had instead filled the sturdy ship with cargo—enough trade goods and supplies to last for a long time.

Mikkel's friend Garth was among those pulling up the anchor. But Garth's brother, his twin—

As Mikkel glanced that way he saw the hate in Hammer's eyes. Like a fist closing around his heart, Mikkel felt the danger. What might that hate cause Hammer to do?

Now his hands were tied behind his back and his feet were tied together. A strong walrus-hide rope lashed him to the ship and kept him from jumping up or over the side. But what if Hammer had one moment of freedom?

Lifting his head, Mikkel looked straight ahead and passed Hammer as if he didn't see him. Yet Mikkel watched out of the corner of his eye. When Hammer shifted his feet, he tried to extend one foot enough to trip him.

Paying no attention, Mikkel walked to the front of the ship. Unlike his own *Conquest*, the smaller longship he had left in Greenland, Leif's *knorr* had places for only twelve oarsmen. Six men sat at the front with three on one side of the bow and three on the other. The remaining six men rowed in the area back of the cargo.

Today Mikkel felt glad that he could row, glad for the strength that had given him this spot. As master of his own ship, he usually stood at the tiller. Since being with Leif, Mikkel had watched and learned from his great skill.

Taking the rowing seat farthest forward, Mikkel sat down on the port, or left side of the ship. Bree's brother Devin sat in the seat across from him. Since leaving Greenland both of them had let their beards grow. With their backs to the bow, each rower waited with his hands on a long oar.

When all was ready, Mikkel leaned forward, lowered the oar, and pulled with the others. Like the rhythm of a song he felt it. Lean forward, lower the oar, pull. Lean forward, lower the oar, pull.

As the ship moved out from the cove, wind filled the great square sail. Soon the men eased back on the oars, and Mikkel turned around to look beyond the bow. The iceberg he had noticed earlier had drifted farther south. Now it lay close to the fjord, near the end of the long wooded coast. Like a blue-white mountain, the iceberg towered above the water.

Facing the stern again, Mikkel looked toward Leif. Tiller in hand, he stood far back on the steering board side of the ship. With steady eyes and a calm face he gazed ahead, watchful and ready.

Seeing him, Mikkel felt relieved. Leif knew what it took to keep a ship safe. He had been the first to warn Mikkel about icebergs. An ice cap—a thick layer of ice and snow—covered a large part of Greenland. When a piece of that glacier broke off, it slid into the ocean and became an iceberg.

While sun and wind melted the top of an iceberg, the ice beneath the surface of the water took longer to melt. Often the jagged points reached out far beyond what could be seen and pierced the hull of a ship.

Nearby, Devin was also watching. "I don't like the look of that iceberg," he said.

"We'll be all right," Mikkel told him with a confidence he didn't feel. But in the next moment he remembered Bjarni, the merchant who had seen these lands, but never stepped foot on them. More than fifteen years later, he gave directions to Leif. And Leif bought this very ship from him.

Mikkel knew the large merchant ship was harder to

handle than his own smaller longship. On their way from
Greenland, Leif had often stayed out at sea to keep from
being driven against the shore. Now he set a wide course
around the iceberg and sailed back in the direction from
which they had come.

We'll be safe, Mikkel told himself again. *Leif knows what
he's doing.*

Just the same, Mikkel looked for Bree. Standing near
the stern, she hung on to the upper edge, or rail of the ship.
At her feet lay the black dog that had followed her from
Norway to Iceland, then to Greenland and onto this ship.

Trust, Mikkel thought, still watching Bree. "I'll prove
I'm worthy of trust," he had promised. But Mikkel felt
sure that she didn't believe him.

More than anyone, Mikkel knew the countless ways
he had hurt Bree, Devin, and the other Irish. Could he
ever leave all that behind? Proving that he could be trusted
would take courage—more courage than he might have.

Sailing across the upwind side, Leif entered the area
between the iceberg and the rugged coast. From where
Mikkel sat he looked beyond Leif to the open sea. Here
and there smaller pieces of ice drifted far enough away to
offer no danger. But then Mikkel caught sight of the sky.
A black cloud lay along the horizon.

Soon the cloud moved up, spreading wide. A cold
wind tore at their clothing. As clouds blotted out the sun,
the blue ocean turned green, then black. Smooth seas

became choppy water and then long swells. Mikkel's muscles tightened with dread.

Mast creaking, ropes taut, men worked to lower the sail. From the long open sea to the north, gusts swept down upon them. High overhead, Leif's banner whipped in the wind.

When the sky grew as dark as a night without stars, Mikkel saw fear in the eyes of seasoned sailors. Every man on board knew what could happen. Needing to run before the wind, they could be driven far off course. Would the squall send them against the rocky coast? or into the iceberg?

Like Mikkel, the other oarsmen were rowing again. Rowing into waves that sloshed over the sides of the ship. With every sweep of the oars Mikkel looked for Bree. With waves high around them she clung to the rail.

Panic filled Mikkel. In one instant she could be swept overboard. "Lie down, Bree!" he shouted. "Hang on to something else!" But Bree didn't turn his way, and Mikkel knew she couldn't hear above the storm.

Tiller in hand, feet braced against the roll of the ship, Leif peered ahead. When the rain came, it slashed against them. Carried on gusts of wind, it pelted like ice.

As the ship dropped into a trough, Mikkel looked up to towering waves. Rowing with all his strength, he and the others worked to turn the bow into the wind. But the wind and current drove them between the iceberg and the land.

Then a gigantic wave crashed into the ship, ran across the deck, and into the cargo hold. Men scrambled for buckets, bailing as fast as they could. On hands and knees, Bree was among them, pouring water over the rail.

Mikkel swallowed hard. *No place for water to run out.* If the ship filled with water, it would sink straight to the bottom.

Dread in his heart, Mikkel felt the current send the ship sideways. What would he do if the iceberg ripped the hull apart?

The next powerful gust picked up the ship, hurling it toward the great white mountain. Forgetting everything else, Mikkel pulled on his oar. With each wave he struggled to head the ship into the wind. With every ounce of strength he rowed to keep the ship away from the iceberg. With every breath he prayed.

As the ship dropped into another deep trough, Mikkel met his greatest fear. Off the end of his oar the water parted. A jagged piece of ice pointed up like a knife.

"Ice to port!" Mikkel shouted as he pulled with all his might.

Around him, the men pulled together. Lean forward. Lower the oar. Pull with all your strength.

With a rhythm born of desperation they rowed. Desperate to win they pulled. Working for their lives they pulled.

Then in one moment it was all over.

THREE

A NEW WORLD

In the center of the ship Bree felt the difference. Unwrapping her arms from the base of the mast, she looked up.

One hand on the tiller, Leif gazed straight ahead. In spite of the danger he had faced, he stood with calm face and eyes filled with courage.

Then the rain eased. As quickly as it came, the cold front passed, and the sea changed again. A strong wind still held the ship in its grasp. The men still rowed, gaining little headway and fighting to keep what they had. But now the wind and current swept them toward shore.

Weak with relief, Bree stood up to look over the side. As Leif sailed around islands in the mouth of the bay, they entered quieter waters. Before long, the wind blew the clouds away.

Leif's warm smile lit his eyes. "Well done, Mikkel. Well done, everyone."

Arms of land reached out to welcome them. On one side lay the long point, extending like a beak into the sea. On the other side, the steep, high ridge of rock. Between the two arms, the ground sloped upward from the waters of the bay.

Like a wave breaking against a shore, excitement ran through the ship. When the bay grew shallow, the men dropped anchor and made ready the small after-boat towed behind the ship. As Leif stepped into the boat, Bree suddenly realized the importance of what she was seeing.

During the voyage from Greenland, Leif had looked across long stretches of barren rock. Naming the area Helluland—Land of Stone Slabs—he told them, "We won't have it said of us, as it was of Bjarni, that we did not go ashore on this land."

At their next stop, Leif looked around and said, "This land shall have a name in keeping with its nature. I call it Markland." Land of Woods.

Now he was going ashore again. Sword at his side and spear in hand, Leif stood at the bow of the small boat. Wearing a green tunic decorated with gold braid, he was easy to see.

When the boat drew close to land, Leif stepped out

into the water. As he waded to shore, water splashed against his knees, then around the leather straps that bound his leggings, and finally over his feet. Walking behind him, Leif's men followed his leading.

From the shore the land rose sharply upward to a terrace eleven or twelve feet above the level of the sea. When Leif stood on the raised bank of earth, he turned. His spear upright and ready, he studied what lay before him.

Beyond the shallow bay, the fjord offered a gateway into a new world. Across that fjord, the wooded coast formed a hazy blue outline in the distance.

Tall and strong, Leif stood there, as though the moment had become part of his dream. For an instant he glanced down at the ground beneath his feet. Then he looked up to the heavens. When Leif smiled, his face shone like the sun coming out from beneath the clouds.

It wasn't long before the boat returned to the ship. Mikkel was rowing. "Come on, Bree," he said. "We want a good meal!"

Bree knew what that meant. Fresh fish or game off the land instead of flat bread and dried fish from their sea chests and barrels.

As men scrambled to get a place in the boat, Mikkel stopped them. "Save room for Dev and Bree. Leif wants her to come and fix salmon for us. We'll have a feast!"

Leif had chosen Bree for the expedition because she was a good cook. Quickly she gathered what she needed. A sharp knife for cleaning fish, a long fork, and then—

"Salmon?" Bree asked.

Mikkel grinned. "So plentiful that I caught one with my bare hands! You'll see!"

As Bree climbed down, the dog that had followed her from Norway leaped onto a barrel, over the side of the ship, and into the boat.

"Shadow!" Bree exclaimed.

Tipping his head, the dog looked at her with beady eyes, but did not move.

"Bad dog!" Bree scolded. Dropping onto his belly, Shadow wagged his tail and crawled partway under a seat.

Oar in hand, Mikkel spoke to her. "Bree, we do not have time to take care of a dog."

"I know." She was embarrassed. In times like this, Shadow made her feel as if she were a child instead of sixteen. Quickly Bree sat down. Wiggling close, Shadow rested his muzzle on her foot. To Bree's surprise Mikkel grinned, then bent to his oar.

On the far side of the terrace stood a forest of balsam fir. As the boat drew closer to shore, one of the men exclaimed, "Look at all those trees!"

After living in Greenland, even the Norwegians among them knew what it meant to be short of wood. From Bree's memory of those three winters came the feel of winds that brought a long season of snow and cold and needing to be sure that both humans and animals had enough food.

Just then five caribou bounded over the open land along the shore. One by one, they leaped across the grassy area. At the edge of the forest a large caribou stopped. In the moment that he turned to look at them, Bree saw the full rack of his antlers.

"Game!" exclaimed one of the men. "Food!" said another.

When they reached shallow water, Bree followed her brother over the side of the boat. As she waded ashore, Bree suddenly stopped, filled with wonder at what she saw. Before her lay a stream that offered fresh drinking water. But there was more.

Mikkel beached the boat and leaped out. "I want to show you the salmon!"

The winding stream tumbled over rocks of all sizes before making a final turn to empty into the bay. Mikkel and Devin wasted no time wading into the water. A short distance beyond them, salmon leaped up a small waterfall.

On his first try Devin caught one with his hands. Holding it up, he called out, "C'mon, Bree. You can do it!"

Like a promise for the new land, his words rang in her ears. The clear water looked inviting. Wading into the stream, Bree reached out for a salmon. When she missed the first one, she grabbed the next. As he fought to get free, she lost her balance.

Gurgling and gasping, Bree picked herself up, but the fish got away. When another salmon came near, Bree guided it into a shallow area near the bank. Moving swiftly, she caught the salmon near the tail and hung on. "I did it!" she called to Devin. "I did it!"

Around her, men turned. When they laughed, Bree didn't care, for they all laughed with her. With long hair streaming down over her eyes, it wasn't hard to imagine how she must look.

When Mikkel didn't hide his grin, she laughed again. "Your salmon is the biggest one yet," he told her.

Her catch was a prize, and Bree knew it. When she climbed out of the stream she showed everyone her fish. Then she found a flat stone and started cleaning it. The salmon was the largest she had ever prepared. She would make the most of her catch.

After finding a safe place for her prize, Bree set out to collect firewood. On her way in from the ship she had noticed huge piles of driftwood. Along one side of the bay she followed the long point of land that reached into the sea.

As the wind caught her long wavy hair, Bree sensed a freedom she hadn't felt for a long time. By now the sea was blue again and the sky free of clouds. From where she stood she looked off to the large island they had climbed that morning. Already Bree thought of it as Current Island because of the strong currents that flowed around it.

Today it seemed a dream that on her thirteenth birthday—nearly four years ago now—she had stood high on the mountain behind her home, thinking, *If only I could know what's out there.*

For Bree the thought had not been new. Years before it started as a hunger, a curiosity about life in distant places. Her curiosity about the world beyond the Irish Sea was a longing that wouldn't go away. It had become her quest.

Never had she realized that she would travel as a Viking slave. And never had she guessed how much she would want to return home. Instead, here she was, joining others in Leif Erikson's expedition to a new world.

When Bree walked back to a place where driftwood had collected, she stood for a moment, awed by the bountiful supply of wood. Here again, God had provided.

For three years Bree had lived in a settlement almost bare of the few trees it once had. When she prepared food she could not allow even one small piece of wood to burn without a reason. And here?

Beyond the grassy land next to the bay, the forest stretched away. Trees for building. Trees for fuel, preparing food, getting dry, and staying warm. And driftwood filled the shores. Washed up with the waves of the sea, it stayed on the land when the tide receded.

Quickly Bree filled her arms. Dry and bleached by the

sun, the driftwood was ready to burn. Her armload of easily gathered wood was another reason to give thanks.

And if she could trust Mikkel—if he really took her and Devin home to Ireland—. But Bree was afraid to hope.

Before leaving, she looked around once more. As she turned to the sea, a whale leaped from the water. For a moment its great body flipped in an arc, then vanished beneath the waves.

Without thinking, Bree spoke aloud. "I like it here."

When the tide was high, Leif brought his ship close to the long point where Bree gathered wood. Her friend Nola found her at once.

Like Bree, Nola had been chosen for the expedition because of her cooking ability. She, too, had been captured by Vikings when Mikkel's men swept through the Wicklow Mountains. On that first dreadful voyage, Bree and Nola had become strong friends. Then when Mikkel's ship reached the Aurland Fjord, Nola met Garth. After setting Nola free, Garth asked her to marry him.

"How can you possibly marry a Norwegian?" Bree had asked when she found out.

Nola only smiled. Soon Bree learned how much she loved Garth. But Hammer was Garth's twin, and the two looked so much alike that Bree also asked, "How can you tell them apart?"

"I've never missed once," Nola told her. But now, three years later, Nola looked toward Hammer with a worried look in her eyes.

During the trip from Greenland, men had tied Hammer's hands and feet so that he could not bring danger to Mikkel again. The same men had untied Hammer's feet so that he could climb out of the ship. Now, as Bree and Nola watched, Leif asked Garth to take off the walrus-hide ropes around Hammer's wrists. Then Leif set him to work on the booths they needed to build.

Soon Bree understood why. Hammer had exceedingly strong arms. On this day he wore a different colored tunic than his twin. Bree could easily tell that Hammer was the one who carved out large pieces of turf—grass-covered dirt—with his knife. As he set the pieces in place to make a wall, Garth never once left his side.

Bree had seen this kind of building at Iceland's *Althing*, the annual meeting of their parliament. The walls of a booth lasted from one year to the next. Men only needed to add wood poles that reached above the turf walls and supported a cloth roof. Before nightfall the booth would be finished, and Leif would have his own shelter. His men would also set up his traveling bed—pieces of wood stored on the ship, ready to fit together when Leif slept on shore.

"Garth knows how much Hammer hates Mikkel," Nola said so quietly that no one but Bree could hear.

"It worries Garth. He tried to protect Mikkel—to protect all of us. But—"

Turning her back on the men, Nola faced the sea. "I'm afraid of Hammer—afraid of his hate—"

"So am I," Bree said. Whenever he looked at Mikkel, Hammer's eyes were full of anger.

As men caught more salmon and brought them to her, Bree cleaned them, but kept watching Hammer. With hands as strong as the biggest hammer, he was well named.

Bree tried to comfort her friend. "Garth is staying right with him." But the worried look did not leave Nola's eyes.

Even now, watching Hammer, a trembling began inside Bree. Would she ever forget that moment when Mikkel passed down a steep slope next to a stream? Would she ever forget Shadow's warning bark? Or seeing Hammer push a rock off a high place onto the path where Mikkel walked?

Six days ago Garth's attempts to protect Mikkel had not been enough. Now everyone waited to see what their leader, Leif, would do.

"I can't forget the hate in Hammer's eyes," Bree whispered.

Though she knew it was impossible, Hammer seemed to have heard her words. When he turned to look at her, the trembling reached into Bree's heart. Her hands started to shake.

THE BIG PLAN

Taking the heavy pot that Bree held, Nola set it down. Then she wrapped her arms around Bree.

As if she were still a little girl and Nola her mother, Bree felt the comfort of strong Irish arms. But when her trembling stopped, Bree asked, "How can I have the courage to win when I'm so scared?"

"Just wait," Nola said. "When you need courage, you'll have it."

"But how can Mikkel act as if nothing is wrong? As though he's not afraid of Hammer?"

Nola's clear gaze met hers. "I think Mikkel *is* afraid. He just doesn't show it. He's Norwegian."

Suddenly both of them laughed. And when Mikkel

brought the salmon he had caught, a wide grin spread across his face. Fresh fish after eating dried cod for what seemed days on end!

As men kept catching salmon, Bree and Nola kept cleaning them. Before long, other men brought the cooking pots from the ship.

On the long trips over the open sea, Bree and Nola used an iron cauldron that hung on a strong chain from a three-legged stand. Within that cauldron they lit a fire and cooked the food inside a smaller pot. But now, as Bree thought about boiling fish again, her stomach turned over.

Again and again she had prepared dried cod from barrels. As if she stood above the cooking water now, she remembered the smell.

"I can't face boiled fish again," she told Devin when he brought the fish he had caught.

Her brother grinned. "How about a meal that celebrates this new land?"

One year older than Bree, Devin had watched out for her from the time they were very young. When they were captured in Mikkel's raid, Devin was set free and then managed to bring ransom for his sister—ransom Bree gave up in order to send two younger girls home to Ireland. But three years had passed since Mikkel promised to give Bree her freedom at the end of the first voyage in his new ship. By now both Mikkel and Devin had sprouted beards and grown tall.

Of the fish Bree and Devin knew in Ireland, salmon was their favorite. Much prized, they considered it superior to all other fish. But how could they cook it in the way it needed to be prepared?

"We need fire pits like the ones in Greenland," Bree said. There she had worked with the women to cook the food most liked by Leif's father, Erik the Red.

Devin hurried to the ship and returned with a wooden shovel. Quickly he dug a round pit in the ground of the terrace. When he finished the first pit, Devin dug a second and then a third. From the shore of the bay he carried the flattest stones he could find to line the bottom of each pit.

While Bree worked, she watched Leif and Mikkel set out. As they started around the bay, they talked without pausing. Whatever they were saying, it seemed really important. Passing between the balsam fir, birch, and alder at the bottom of the rocky ridge, they climbed the steep slope to the top. Though they were off in the distance, Bree could still see the green cloth of Leif's tunic against the sky.

Partway across the rocky ridge, he stopped, looked off to the sea, and then turned to study the bay and the area around the terrace. He was planning, Bree felt sure.

Looking at the site from all angles with every possibility in mind.

Then he and Mikkel disappeared, dropping down on the far side of the ridge to the channel. Already men called it Straumfjord or Current Fjord.

When he returned from talking with Leif, Mikkel was upset.

"What's wrong?" Devin asked when Mikkel stopped to talk with him and Bree.

"Leif told me I would be a key to what happens to Hammer. I don't want to be a key. Hammer has done one thing after another to hurt me. When he pushed that rock—"

As Bree looked at Devin, she saw that his face had gone blank. Not one blink of an eyelash showed what he was thinking, but Bree felt sure that she knew. Much as both of them hated all the things Hammer had done to harm Mikkel, Mikkel's raid on the Irish countryside had changed their lives forever. Mikkel had done one thing after another to hurt them and their family.

"Did Leif tell you anything else?" Devin asked.

"He said, 'Remember my father.'"

When Devin smiled the light came back into his eyes. Everyone in the Norse world—the world of men from the North—knew what had happened to Erik the Red. Known for his red hair and fiery temper, Erik was out-lawed from Iceland because of his crimes. Sent off alone, he could have perished on the open sea. Instead, he found Greenland and explored it for three years.

At the end of his time of being outlawed, Erik returned to Iceland. There he gathered together a group of people who settled the new land. Now, more than fifteen years later, he continued to be the leader of those settlements.

"Leif said, 'Remember my father'?" Devin asked quietly.

"I would say, 'Remember Leif's mother.'" Bree spoke just as softly. During her time in Greenland she had grown to love Leif's mother. Bree felt sure she had been the one who taught Leif to be wise and even-tempered in the way he handled difficult things.

Mikkel looked from Devin to Bree. "I don't like what you're saying."

"I hear the whispers," Bree answered. "When King Olaf asked Leif to bring Christianity to Greenland, people wondered if he had any choice. Leif himself told the king that it would be difficult to do. But when he got to Greenland, Leif talked to his mother and she believed in the God Leif talked about. She even built the first Christian church in Greenland. How would that happen if Leif wasn't wise in what he told her?"

But Mikkel was still upset. "I'm not Leif. I'm not some big important leader."

"Someday you will be." Devin spoke with a certainty that Mikkel could not ignore.

"All right," he said. "But I don't trust Hammer. I don't dare turn my back to him. And I don't want to help him. He won't ever change."

"Really?" Bree's voice sounded like milk and honey. She didn't like Hammer either. Instead she was terrified of him. But in that moment there was something Bree knew. She was even more afraid of what might happen to him. "Hammer won't ever change?"

Mikkel stared at her. "You are defending Hammer after he nearly killed me?"

"No, I'm trying to believe he can change."

"So you're telling *me* what to do?" Mikkel asked. "You aren't acting like a slave."

"That's true. I will *never* make a good slave. So if you want me to trust you, why don't you keep your promises? Take us back to Aurland? Set me free?"

Without another word Mikkel whirled around and stalked away.

As Bree and Nola prepared the late-day meal, men lowered the sail onto the supports at the center of the ship. Spreading out the large piece of cloth, they lashed the edges to the oar ports on the sides of the ship. There Bree, Nola, and many of the others would live until the men built houses.

"Our bed is ready," Nola told Bree as Leif's men finished tying down the sail. "If it rains again, we'll have a dry place to go."

When Bree built a fire inside the cooking pits, she allowed the wood to burn, then pushed the embers to the side of the heated stones. After wrapping wet leaves around the salmon, she laid them inside the pits. Finally she covered the openings with hot stones, then embers, then a big piece of sod.

Soon the aroma of baking salmon rose around them. When the food was ready, the men gathered quickly, eager for a freshly caught meal. Some dropped down on the ground, while others such as Leif sat on a sea chest his men brought from the ship. Bree still wanted to make the most of the fish she had caught.

Usually the men held out their wooden bowls, and she and Nola filled them. But for Leif? To break up such a magnificent salmon and fit pieces into a bowl? Besides, this should be a celebration.

As Bree looked around, she found the smooth wooden cover of a large barrel. Quickly she cleaned it. When all was ready, she took her big salmon from the cooking pit, carefully laid it out, and presented it proudly.

When Bree set the perfectly baked salmon before Leif, he looked up with gratitude. "You've prepared a fitting feast for a new land."

Bree smiled. "Eat it fast so it stays warm," she wanted to say. But as she started away to dish up food for the others, Leif's words held her there. "Just wait."

When he bowed his head, Leif was silent for a

moment. As he spoke, his voice was filled with gratitude. "Our Father, we couldn't see Your footprints, but Your path led through the sea, Your way through the mighty waters. Thank You for Your protection—for bringing us safely to this good land."

Again Leif paused, as though thinking about all they would need in the days ahead. His request was simple. "Help us to be wise in how we use the abundance of this new world."

As soon as they finished eating, Leif looked from one person to the next as if feeling the importance of this moment. When he laid out his plan, his voice held the strength he showed in everything he did.

"This land will make us grow. We cannot come into something so big, so important, and so abundant without having it change us."

As Bree listened, she felt the power of Leif's voice. Then she knew something more. As leader of the expedition, he understood better than anyone the uncertainties they faced. Yet the almost certain dangers didn't frighten him.

"Each of you has been chosen because you have a special skill." As Leif looked around the group, his gaze stopped at the Scottish slave couple he had brought from Norway. When King Olaf Tryggvason asked Leif to bring Christianity to Greenland, he told him to use Haki and Hekja if he ever needed speed, for they could run as fast as deer.

"Early tomorrow morning start on a three-day journey," Leif told the couple. "Run through the land and come back and report what you see."

Already Bree knew the woman, Hekja, from their time together in Greenland. Bree had no doubt that her good Irish mother would be offended by the clothing Hekja wore, for it ended well above her knee.

"Aren't you cold?" Bree sometimes asked during the long winters. As Hekja shook her head, her blue eyes filled with laughter. Only when the fiercest winds blew did she pull a warm animal skin around her. On days like this when the sun was warm, Bree often wished that she, too, could run without wearing a long skirt.

For a moment Leif's gaze rested on Nola's husband, Garth, then on Hammer, Garth's twin. As Bree glanced that way, she again saw the anger in Hammer's eyes—an anger quickly hidden when he stared down at his feet.

Leif cleared this throat. "We know that Hammer willfully endangered Mikkel's life—"

"And us all," murmured a Norwegian next to Bree.

But Leif went on. "We need to consider his punishment. If you Norwegians were home, or if we were in Iceland or Greenland, we'd have a meeting of our assembly. The *ting* would decide what to do. I ask you who are free men to think about this problem. Three days from now we'll vote to decide Hammer's fate."

Leif paused, and again looked around the group. "When the time comes to go home, I want every one of you along, safe and well. That means we need to work together every day and every minute. I expect you to work as teams. Sometimes you'll have to change who you're with to fit what you're doing. But you always have a responsibility to look out for one another."

Starting around the circle, Leif paired each person with someone else. Garth with his wife Nola. Devin with a man from Greenland. The Scottish couple, Haki and Hekja, with each other. Each time Leif named his choice, Bree agreed. But then Leif told Mikkel to take care of her. Bree's temper flared.

The day before she was captured in Mikkel's raid, Bree had saved him from drowning. "You owe me something," she told him when she found herself on his ship. Instead of letting her go, Mikkel had promised to watch out for her. Sometimes Bree had needed his protection. At other times she felt as if she were suffocating.

Now, after coming to this new world, she had started to dream again about what it would mean to be free. She didn't want *anyone*, especially Mikkel, to remind her that she was still a slave. Besides, she could take care of herself!

But when Bree met Mikkel's gaze, he only grinned.

"Don't forget," she said later when Leif couldn't hear.

"I'm supposed to watch out for you. If you make life hard for me, I'll put stones in your food."

"You can do that," Mikkel answered calmly. "But if you do, I'll make sure that Leif is watching. And I'll look at you when I spit out the stones one by one."

FIVE

DANGER IN THE FOREST

When Mikkel got up the next morning, he saw Leif stepping off distances on the terrace. Garth was with him, putting down stakes.

Three large houses. Mikkel felt sure of it. And maybe additional buildings. Leif was thinking big. If this was to be a gateway—a stopping place for people coming from long distances—there would need to be room to house them. And plenty of room to store trade goods coming in and going out.

Watching Leif plan, Mikkel looked forward to what lay ahead. Could this land ever be home? Again he thought about it. With each new discovery he felt excitement deep in his spirit. But then—

As soon as their early meal ended, all of Mikkel's good thoughts fell into a deep hole.

"I'll make my final decision about this site when Haki and Hekja get back," Leif said. "But we need to get ready for winter and can't waste even one day. If Thorstein gets here—"

As if wondering where his brother was, Leif looked across the bay to the fjord of strong currents. Like a gigantic white sail an iceberg drifted past, a reminder to all of them.

Leif started again. "*When* Thorstein comes, our work crew will more than double."

Quickly Leif divided up what needed to be done. Some would stay here, repairing the ship. Others would hunt and fish, and the women would dry salmon for winter. Still others would chop down trees they could use to build here or take wherever needed.

With few remaining trees in Greenland, Leif was quick to choose men from Norway because of their experience in cutting timber.

"Garth, I want you to walk through the forest. Mark the trees that would make the best poles." Other men would follow, chopping down the trees. And Mikkel and Hammer would work together.

Work together? Mikkel couldn't believe what he was hearing. Had Leif forgotten what Hammer had done? Only seven days had passed since what could have been a deadly accident. In less than two days they would decide whether to outlaw Hammer—whether to send him off alone into the great unknown.

The forest of balsam fir grew close behind the terrace. As the men headed for the trees, Mikkel fell into step with his friend Garth. A farmer in Aurland, the Norwegian fjord where Mikkel's family lived, Garth was also a skillful carpenter.

Mikkel had always liked being with him. Though the twins looked exactly alike, Garth talked more and often told stories about the brave deeds of mighty men. But Hammer was different. When Mikkel said something to him, Hammer just nodded or shook his head and kept walking.

The moment Hammer was out of earshot, Mikkel's anger spilled over. "How can Leif do this to me?" he asked Garth. "Your brother—your twin—is a dangerous man. He wants to hurt—even kill me!"

Mikkel stopped, drew a deep breath. He was so upset he could barely speak. When he did, his anger came through every word.

"One minute Leif says we have to decide what to do with Hammer. The next Leif gives me the dangerous job of working with him. Chopping down trees of all things!"

"Watch your back," Garth answered.

"Watch my back! Stay completely away from him, you mean."

"I've tried everything I know to get Hammer to talk to me," Garth said. "Ever since your voyage to Ireland he's hated you, but he won't say what's wrong."

It worried Mikkel. Like a pot of water over a low fire, Hammer's anger had simmered for a long time. After three peaceful years in Greenland, Mikkel had thought the threat of danger had passed. Then Hammer had seen a chance to get even. He took it.

Why had Hammer's anger come to a boil a week ago? Why had he suddenly tried to do his worst?

Now Mikkel tried to push away the uneasiness he felt. But then Garth asked the very question that Mikkel wanted to ignore. "When will Hammer try to hurt you again?"

As they started up the hill behind the terrace, Hammer walked with the other men. Careful to stay out of his way, Mikkel dropped still farther back. Judging by the set of his shoulders, Hammer was even more angry than usual. It wasn't hard to guess that he didn't want to work with Mikkel.

But then Mikkel saw his chance. When Hammer was a short distance away from the other men, Mikkel spoke to his back. "I know why you hate me."

Hammer whirled around. "No, you don't."

"I do," Mikkel answered. "I know why you want revenge."

"So what are you going to do about it? Be the great

Viking? Master of a ship—the merchant who travels the far seas?"

Mikkel stared at him. How could he possibly work with this man? Why had Leif asked this of him? Mikkel couldn't think of anything that would be more dangerous. He dreaded even the thought of it.

As the others walked on, Mikkel stopped and looked back. From where he stood, the ground sloped down to the bay. Here, at an opening between trees, the morning air felt fresh and cool. Mikkel welcomed it.

Then he thought of Leif's words. "Remember my father."

"Remember Leif's mother," Bree had added. The worst of it was that Bree was too often right.

Mikkel tried to toss it off, pushing aside her words, but it didn't work. Because of his raid, Bree had become a slave. Yet from the moment he met her, he had never been able to ignore what she said.

"Hammer won't ever change?" Bree had turned Mikkel's words into a question.

By the time Mikkel caught up to the other men, he felt uneasy right down to his toes. *If I don't think Hammer can change, how can I change enough to be trusted?*

Garth had stopped and now he kept looking up, studying the trees to decide which ones would be best. Each support pole needed to be straight, thick, and strong, and they would need many more poles for each roof.

As soon as Garth marked a number of trees, he walked on, and the other men followed. Mikkel and Hammer stayed behind and started to work.

Without a word, Hammer began trimming the lower branches of the first tree. With each stroke of his powerful arms, his ax chipped through the wood. Watching him, Mikkel felt fascinated by his strength. Then he felt afraid.

What was Leif doing sending him out in the woods with such a man? The strokes of Hammer's ax seemed to come from a fire deep inside. How could Mikkel possibly trust him? When felling a tree, a man's life could depend on the person with whom he worked.

Then as Mikkel trimmed branches on a different tree he changed his mind. If he wanted to learn from someone, Hammer was the person. Not one stroke of his ax was wasted. As the morning wore on, Mikkel learned to admire his single-minded ability to work.

From the time he was a young boy, Mikkel had gone into the wooded areas of their mountains with his father. Early on, he had learned a respect for safety, and he knew exactly which men worked well. Like them, Hammer always knew which way a tree would fall.

Before long, Mikkel made it a game. "Point," he told Hammer. "Tell me where you're going to drop it, and I'll watch it go."

Each time Mikkel finished trimming the lower

branches, he cleared them away from the base. With each new balsam fir Hammer looked up, studying the tree. Sometimes he walked around it, still looking up.

Lifting his hand, Hammer pointed to the exact place where the tree would fall. Then he made his first wedge-shaped cut. Still using his ax he chopped his way around the tree, shaping the trunk as if he were a beaver. By midday Hammer had called every tree right.

"How do you do it?" Mikkel exclaimed. When Hammer grinned, the tension between them suddenly vanished.

That morning Bree and Nola had sent along a between-meals snack. Mikkel and Hammer sat down on one of the logs to enjoy their food. When they started again, Hammer told him, "This time you drop the trees." Before long, it was Hammer who said, "You call it. I'll watch it go."

By now they had dropped enough trees to see the islands beyond the bay. Here and there they had left trees to grow, but they could feel the air off the water. The long trunks that would become poles waited on the ground for men to carry them out.

While Hammer cleared away the branches he had trimmed, Mikkel studied yet another tree. To his surprise Hammer had showed him how to like what they were doing, and Mikkel took his time. As he circled the tree, looking up, he felt a change in the air.

Stopping, he waited. In the open space with most of

the trees gone, he felt a gust of wind. Even a wind much smaller than the one that caught their ship could affect the way a tree fell.

"Call it!" Hammer said as he returned from throwing branches in a pile. His face was open now and he looked pleased about the work they had done. But Mikkel set down his ax.

"I can't," he said. "The wind has come up. I don't want to take a chance on hurting you."

As though suddenly turning to ice, Hammer froze. All expression drained out of his face. But then he chose to ignore Mikkel's words.

"It's not that big a wind. Here, I'll show you."

Looking up, Hammer studied the tree, chopped his first wedge-shaped cut, and then chopped his way around the trunk. As Mikkel watched, he felt another change in the air.

Cold, he thought. Again he felt uneasy. The sun still shone, but the squall that struck the ship was still too fresh in his mind. Then, just as the fir started to waver, a gust of wind caught the branches, spinning the tree toward Hammer.

"Run!" Mikkel shouted. But the ring of Hammer's ax covered the warning. Racing forward, Mikkel pushed him hard, shoving Hammer out of the way. An instant later Mikkel felt the sting of something hitting his face. Then he forgot everything else. With a great thud the tree crashed on the ground not far from Hammer.

As the branches quivered and settled, Hammer lay there stunned. Then slowly he picked himself up. On his feet again, he faced Mikkel. "I hate you."

Mikkel stared at him. All morning long they had worked together in peace. Why was Hammer angry now?

Once again his eyes held resentment. "So. Why the big rescue? You still want to be the great Viking?"

Mikkel couldn't believe what he was hearing. "Are you serious?"

"They'll take me out to the farthest island they can find. A rocky island with no trees or grass or food. Not even birds' eggs to eat. They'll leave me without a ship— not even a small boat. I won't have any way to get any- where."

"What are you talking about?" Mikkel asked.

"Why didn't you let me die? One quick death instead of long, slow starvation."

Suddenly Mikkel understood. "The meeting of the free men. Their vote to decide your punishment."

Slowly Hammer nodded his head up and down. "And I am done for."

"No! They've got to talk about it."

"Talk about it if *you* had done something. Not if *I* do something. Don't forget who you are—son of the mighty chieftain of the Aurland Fjord!"

An angry red flushed Hammer's face. "Remember? My punishment will be bigger because of who you are. And now they'll say that Hammer tried again."

"What do you mean?" As much as Mikkel had disliked this man, all that had changed. For the first time he had seen Hammer as someone he could respect. "You didn't hurt me."

Hammer's laugh was cold, and hard, and bitter. "Feel your cheek, Mikkel. The end of a branch must have hit you going down."

Mikkel felt his short, close-to-his-chin beard. Then above it, between his eye and his hair. To his surprise his fingers came away with blood on them.

"It's just a scratch," Mikkel said.

"A scratch that will be my life."

"I'll tell them it wasn't your fault." Mikkel picked up his ax and started away.

But Hammer's voice followed him. "Who are you to talk so big, you who led a raid on innocent people?"

Mikkel turned back. When he answered, his voice was quiet. "I am someone who is sorry for what he did."

Turning again, Mikkel walked away. In that moment everything seemed upside down. Leif was right. He, Mikkel, did hold the key to what happened to Hammer.

To make things even worse, Mikkel had to be honest with himself. Though Hammer didn't want to talk about it, Mikkel did know the reason for his hate. For the first time since Mikkel understood that reason, he forgot to cover his back.

When Mikkel walked out of the forest he saw Bree kneeling by the stream, filling two buckets with water. As he drew close, she looked up.

"Your face!" she exclaimed. "What happened?"

Again Mikkel felt his beard, then the long sensitive line between his right eye and his hair. Looking at his fingers, he shrugged. "Less blood now."

"It's starting to dry. I'll wash it for you. This water is clean and you'll heal better."

Years ago her mother had taught Bree everything she knew about taking care of wounds. As Mikkel leaned over the stream, she dipped her hand in the water and washed the long scratch. "What did Hammer do?"

"Nothing!"

"You're sure?" she asked.

"I'm sure."

"You're not just saying that?"

"It wasn't his fault. It was one of those things—"

"One of those things that happens when you're cutting trees?"

Mikkel nodded.

"You could have lost your eye."

"But I didn't. It wasn't Hammer's fault."

"Hold still," she told him as she finished washing. "No one will believe that, you know."

Mikkel sighed. "I know."

When he sat up again, he felt surprised at the sympathy in Bree's eyes. In that moment he didn't want to talk about Hammer anymore.

"From the time I met you I knew there was something special about you," Mikkel told her. "I thought it was your God."

"It is."

"But it's also your family."

"Yes."

"They taught you to live with courage."

"And to care so deeply for each other that when we're apart we long to be together."

"Does that ever leave room for anyone else?"

The question startled Bree. "What do you mean?"

"What if—" When Mikkel stopped, Bree waited, watching him, but he did not go on.

"What if what?" she asked.

Mikkel looked away. Beyond the islands in the mouth of the bay, sunlight shone on the blue waters of Current Fjord. But Bree knew that beneath the surface the current ran strong and swift and dangerous.

Then Mikkel's gaze met hers. "What if someone loved you and couldn't be part of your family?"

SIX

HAMMER'S FATE

U nable to speak, Bree stared at Mikkel. The pounding of her heart seemed so loud that she felt sure
he could hear it.

When she answered she could barely utter the words.
"From the time I was a little girl I've dreamed about the
man I would someday wed. It never occurred to me that
I might have to choose between him and my family."

"And what if you had to make that choice?" Mikkel's
voice was low as if he, too, found it difficult to speak.

"I don't know, Mikkel. I don't think I can."

Unable to face the possibility of it, Bree jumped up.
Clutching her buckets of water, she headed back to the

place where she and Nola cooked. To her relief Mikkel did not follow her.

She felt upset, just thinking about what it would mean if her family didn't love and accept the person she wanted to marry. Mikkel was a Christian now. He had turned away from his pagan gods. Bree felt grateful for that choice. But what would happen if he ever went back to Ireland?

Bree knew without doubt how her neighbors and friends would feel. And her family.

From the time she was old enough to think about the person she would wed, Bree had cherished a dream in her heart. The man she loved would talk with her father about whether he could marry her. They would agree on what he should bring to the marriage and her father would give his permission. How could she possibly shut her family out of such an important choice as a husband?

And there was something else. From the beginning, Mikkel had cared more about fame and fortune than about what happened to others. Why else would he lead a raid on the Glendalough Monastery? The gems and other gifts brought by pilgrims to the monasteries were well known to Vikings. Now Mikkel was sorry about what he had done, but—

Mikkel still held one dark secret to himself. A secret known only to Bree, her brother Devin, and one person in Dublin. What would happen if Mikkel found out that she and Dev had discovered the truth?

Bree shivered. Like a warm thought on a cold night, she remembered the close relationship between her mother and father. No dark secrets between them. Honesty and good talk. And when they had a need they prayed together.

That's what she wanted. To be able to believe in the man she wed. To trust and respect him. To know he would be honest with her and with God.

Now, as Bree looked off to the sea, she felt the wind on her face and knew what to do. She would be polite to Mikkel, but that was all. As a slave, she had no choice but to be polite. And Mikkel had watched out for her. More than once he'd protected her from something that would have harmed her. But she would keep him out of any part of her thinking.

That would take care of the problem. Besides, wasn't Tully the one she hoped to wed? All she had to do was see Tully again and everything would be all right.

It would be simple to shut Mikkel out. She would get used to that emptiness now so that later—

Later. Later what?

I will get home, she promised herself. And if Tully hasn't learned to care about someone else—

Filled with hurt at even the thought of it, Bree pushed her dread aside. But it came back. Nearly four years had passed since the Vikings stole her away from

Ireland. Tully had never promised he would wait for her. She had been too young to talk of marriage, but they had always been friends. *Tully, and Dev, and me.*

Bree couldn't fool herself. Friends. The three of them. Childhood friends.

Tully, my brother's friend.

But hadn't Tully's cousin, Lil, who was also captured by Vikings, said more than once that he wanted to marry Bree? Or was she just imagining things because she wanted to go home? Go home to something safe, and secure, and same?

Same.

For the rest of the day Bree thought about it. *Same.* As in *nothing ever changes*? Always there, to be counted on. Would that be good or bad?

The next day Haki and Hekja returned in time for the late meal. "We're standing at the top of a long and wide peninsula," Haki told them. "We ran one day's journey down its side. Then we crossed over." Pointing with his hand, Haki seemed to draw a line from east to west. "We came back along the fjord of currents."

Turning, Haki looked out across the bay to the swiftly flowing fjord they called Straumfjord or Current Fjord.

"How long is the fjord?" Leif asked quickly.

"We saw no end. It goes deep into the land—as far

as we went. We saw rivers full of fish. Forests full of game. This is a rich land with many trees and birds and animals. But we saw no people."

"No one lives in such a good land?" Leif asked.

"No one for three days' journey. We looked for signs of men who fish or hunt. We looked for boats and cooking fires. In boggy ground we looked for footprints. We saw no one."

Leif did not seem surprised. Instead, he told them his decision at once.

"I've chosen the locations for three houses and have planned what we need for each one. Tomorrow morning we'll begin building."

Leif looked around the group. "Now, those of you who are free men. We must decide what to do about Hammer. By his actions he endangered Mikkel's life. What should be his fate?"

As the men talked, Hammer's face looked cold and hard. Instead of being filled with hate, his eyes lacked any expression at all. Bree wondered which was worse.

One man after another stood to speak. "Hammer deserves to be outlawed," said the first. "Leif sent Mikkel and Hammer out to work together, and look what happened to Mikkel!"

From where he sat on his sea chest Mikkel suddenly straightened. In the remaining light of day the scratch on his cheek looked an angry red. Then, instead of speaking, he waited.

"We have no extra ship," the next man said. "Not even a small boat to send Hammer out. If we take him far from here and leave him on the land, he could walk back. If we bring him to a distant island we must have no doubt that he deserves death."

"He deserves death, all right!" said still another. "There's no doubt in our minds that Hammer tried to kill Mikkel. And Mikkel is the son of the mighty chieftain of Aurland Fjord."

The next man mentioned an additional crime. "We need Mikkel's ability to build and repair ships. When Hammer tried to harm Mikkel, he brought danger to us all."

Off to one side of the group Bree, Devin, and Nola sat on the ground. One by one, Bree watched the men and listened as they spoke. Each was more upset than the last. As she felt their anger growing, Bree had no doubt that Hammer would be separated from them and sent out to die.

One moment she didn't want that to happen. The next moment her fear of Hammer took over. She felt so concerned for Mikkel that she wanted Hammer gone, never part of their expedition again. It would be a relief.

Bree had seen for herself what Hammer could do. Would she ever forget the terrible moment when she looked up to see the hate in his eyes? Just thinking about it, Bree trembled.

As though understanding her thoughts, Nola put an arm around her shoulders. Bree drew a long, deep breath, but her fear of Hammer did not go away. He had acted outside the law. How could they do anything else but outlaw him?

Elbows on his knees, Hammer's twin brother, Garth, sat on his sea chest. The palms of his hands supported his bowed head. Through all the speeches he did not look up once.

Finally after the other free men had spoken, only Garth and Mikkel remained. When Leif asked Garth if he wanted to say something, he shook his head. Mikkel stood up.

"First, I want to set something straight." Mikkel touched his cheek. "This is not Hammer's fault. It happened to me, as it could happen to any of you, when we were chopping down a tree.

"For what happened before we reached this land, do we send Hammer away from us? We all know that if we were in our home countries we would not hesitate to outlaw him. We would decide on the length of time and send him away. He would be unable to see his relatives, neighbors, and friends until his time of outlawry was up. If he returned before the end of that time, he could be instantly killed.

"But we've already said there is no extra ship for Hammer to use. There's no small boat he can take. If we put him on an island out at sea there's no way for him to return when his time is up. And if we send him to the land we're on, he could walk back without warning.

"So, do we send Hammer out to die? Some of you believe he's worthy of that. One of you said that you need me, but if we're honest about it, we all need each other. Until Thorstein comes, we're thirty-five men in a strange land. Without Hammer, we're thirty-four."

Mikkel looked from one free man to the next. "This is what I propose—a mercy that will help us all. We need Hammer's strong arms and his skills. We need his ability to drop trees and lift heavy timbers. I propose that he stays here under the watchful eye of his brother and of us all. If he lives with fairness and safety for everyone, he can remain. If he does not, he'll be sent away—taken three days' journey by ship and left on an island without food."

As Mikkel sat down a thoughtful smile spread across Leif's face. "Well said," he told Mikkel. "What do the rest of you say?"

Bree looked at her brother. "When did Mikkel grow up?" she whispered. "He sounds like his father, Sigurd."

Devin grinned. "The mighty chieftain of the Aurland Fjord."

As Leif and the other free men talked about Mikkel's words, they saw that his proposal was wise. When the vote was taken, the free men agreed. As long as Hammer took care to harm no one, and as long as he did a good day's work, he would be allowed to stay.

His gaze strong and steady, Leif charged Hammer with the seriousness of what he had done. "If you do not fulfill your side of the agreement you can be instantly killed. Or you will be taken to the place we decide, and we will leave you. There will be no second chance."

SEVEN

MIKKEL'S PROMISE

As Devin walked to the ship, he kicked a stone ahead of him. Not since he was a young boy had he done that. Now he felt pleased every time the stone landed where he wanted. It seemed much easier than what was happening in his life. He wished it would be just as easy to push aside the way he felt.

He didn't like having Leif tell Mikkel to take care of Bree. And Bree take care of Mikkel? He had seen her wash Mikkel's face at the stream, then walk quickly away. It wasn't like Bree to suddenly leave like that. She had to be upset, and Devin thought he knew why. And now, tonight—

Devin sighed. He wanted Bree to be able to respect

Mikkel. He, too, wanted to respect Mikkel. After all they had been through, it would be good for both of them to watch Mikkel become a strong leader. And as Bree said, Mikkel had sounded like his father, Sigurd. His wise, kind, and good father, Sigurd.

But Mikkel wasn't Sigurd. And it wasn't hard to notice how Mikkel felt about Bree.

Along the shore of the bay, Devin stopped. It was too early to go onto the crowded ship. He would never be able to sleep. Besides, he needed to think. From the time they were very young, Devin had been the older brother, watching out for Bree. That wasn't going to change now. But what could he do?

As the stars began coming out, Devin started walking to the far side of the bay. Already he knew the best way to go, and when the moon rose above the water, it would be easier yet.

He was deep in thought when he heard someone running in the darkness. *Mikkel*, Devin decided. On their second day there, Mikkel had started running when he had a free moment. It was as if he raced against himself, always trying to get faster. But now he slowed to a walk and fell into step beside Devin.

"Good job tonight," Devin told him. "You sounded like your father, Sigurd."

Mikkel stopped dead in his tracks. "You think so?"

"I know so. You figured out what would be best for

Hammer and for the rest of us. Leif was pleased. Bree noticed it too."

"She did?" Mikkel sounded hopeful.

"She did. She even told me so."

Mikkel laughed. "You don't have to lie to me, Dev. Both of us know what Bree really thinks of me. Quite often she'd like to spit in my face."

"I'm not lying."

"Thanks, Dev." Mikkel spoke quietly, and Devin knew that he meant it. Their relationship had been filled with one quarrel after another, but gradually they had started respecting one another.

"We've been friends a long time now," Mikkel said. "But enemies first—"

It was Mikkel who had once asked, "Be my friend, Dev." His request had surprised Devin, and then he understood it was much more. The brother with whom Mikkel felt closest had gone down at sea.

"Big enemies—" Mikkel said. "But now—"

As though remembering all the hard times they had walked through, Mikkel fell silent. Around the bay they walked, neither of them speaking. By the time they reached the far end, the moon had risen enough for Devin to see Mikkel's face. And now he knew what to say.

But Mikkel spoke first. "Dev, who is Tully?"

"Bree never told you?"

"All I know is what I overheard. The young Irish girl

Lil—the one who ran away with Bree—told her that Tully wants to marry her."

So, Devin thought. He had been right, after all. That was why Mikkel waited in Greenland, not taking Bree home.

"Bree never explained?" Devin asked.

When Mikkel shook his head, Devin kept walking. "Then I won't either. You'll have to ask her."

Soon after he reached the Aurland Fjord with Bree's ransom, Devin had been thrown in jail. All winter he waited for the meeting of the *ting,* the parliamentary group that would decide his fate. As he waited, Devin was allowed out of jail during the day to make rivets for the ship Mikkel was building. The two started to talk and gradually became friends.

When the *ting* set Devin free, he was able to return to Ireland. But instead of taking Bree, Devin planned to take two younger girls—their sister Keely, who had been captured in an earlier raid, and Bree's friend Lil. That's when Mikkel had struck a bargain.

"Devin, if you come back from Ireland, and if you and Bree go with me on the first voyage of my new ship, I'll set her free when we return to Aurland," he promised.

Now Devin took a deep breath. No matter what it cost, he was determined to be honest. "Mikkel, you and I have become friends. But I don't want you taking care of my sister."

Stopping again, Mikkel faced Devin. "Leif told me to take care of her. And a long time ago I promised Bree I'd watch out for her."

Devin shook his head. "It's my job now. I'm her brother. I'm here, and I'll take care of her like I always have."

"But Leif teamed you up with a man from Greenland."

"I know. I'll do both."

In the light of the moon Devin looked full into Mikkel's face. He had grown tall in these years. His shoulders were wide and strong, and his blond beard trimmed close to his chin. He was becoming the leader he would be in his own country.

Devin tried again. "Mikkel, you know that I really *am* your friend—that I believe you've changed. You still have some things to work out, but you've changed."

Gratitude filled Mikkel's eyes. "Thanks, Dev—"

But Devin wasn't finished. "That's why I hope you'll understand something."

Mikkel stepped back, his eyes wary and waiting.

"You promised to take us home."

Mikkel nodded.

"A thousand times you've promised, and you haven't done it. You always say, 'It's still one voyage.'"

One voyage. Devin knew it had been Mikkel's way of getting what he wanted. He had stayed in Greenland, putting off his trip home for three years.

But now Mikkel surprised Devin. "I wanted both of you along so you could pray to your God," Mikkel said. "I thought that if you prayed, my ship and crew would be safe."

As Mikkel started walking again, he looked out across the bay. In the moonlight the water lapped gently at the shore, but to Devin waves seemed to crash against his heart.

"You know our God now," he said. "You can pray for yourself. You haven't taken us home—you've delayed all this time because you're really hoping—"

Mikkel turned to him. "You don't have to say it. We understand each other."

"If Bree and I ever *do* get home, she needs to come back to our family—our life there—"

Devin paused and then put it straight. "She needs to marry an Irish lad."

When Mikkel spoke again, it sounded as if he were choking. "I know, Dev. But I don't want to think about it."

"I don't want you to marry my sister. You took her away from our family once. And as the son of a great Norwegian chieftain, you're expected to marry a certain kind of girl. If you married Bree, where would you live?"

Again Mikkel looked across the bay. "I don't know, Dev. I wish it could be here."

But Devin refused to listen to him.

"Because you led that raid, Bree has lost four years of her life being a slave. Do you want to be fair to her? To be honest with yourself?"

Mikkel sighed. "We have to do what Leif says, so I'll watch out for Bree. But I'll watch from a distance."

Turning quickly, he walked away. In the moonlight Devin saw that Mikkel's usual confidence had gone out of his steps. When he and Bree first met him, Mikkel had been prideful and arrogant. Then slowly he changed. But it was the first time Devin saw him walk with a bowed head. And his shoulders had a definite slump.

Then suddenly he turned back. In spite of Devin's hurtful words, Mikkel grinned. "Let's *both* take care of Bree. She gets in so much trouble she'll probably need both of us."

Mikkel was right. When Devin laughed, the tension between them disappeared. "But remember—" Devin said.

"I understand how you feel," Mikkel said quickly. "I'll watch Bree from a distance."

EIGHT

SHADOW

The next morning Mikkel was part of the crew that started building Leif's house. As Garth watched the first row of sod being laid, he spoke quietly to Mikkel.

"If you see anyone doing anything that isn't safe—"

Mikkel nodded. Garth felt even more concerned than he did about what Hammer might do. Today he and some of the other men carried long trunks of balsam fir from the forest. Near the site of Leif's house they worked together, stripping the bark.

Others cut turf, using their sharp knives to slice through the grass and a thick layer of dirt. Laying one piece of sod after another, they built long, solid walls.

Working together, Garth and Mikkel built square

frames and the covers that would be needed for smoke holes in the roof. Next they shaped the long poles for opening and closing those covers from the inside. In everything he did, Mikkel used the skills he had mastered in building his own longship.

And always he and Garth were watching. Trying to avoid what might go wrong.

Day by day Garth counted the poles that were ready. "Three houses," he said.

The buildings required eighty-six large trees for support posts with about forty poles just for Leif's house. Then they needed still more poles for the roof beams, as well as wood to panel the walls and build the platforms used as sitting and sleeping benches.

"If winter comes as early as in Greenland—"

In Greenland there was no choice but to be ready for winter. When the winds howled down upon them, shelter was a matter of life or death. But right now something else bothered Mikkel much more. His promise to Devin.

Watch Bree from a distance? With her ability to attact danger, it was the worst promise he could possibly make.

When he saw Bree pick up two buckets and head for the forest, Mikkel groaned. Why had Leif given him, of all people, the impossible task of looking after Bree?

Mikkel put down his ax, but knew he had to be careful. If there was anything Bree wanted, it was her freedom. And she didn't want anyone, especially him, to hinder her right to walk about as she pleased. What's more, on this day Mikkel was supposed to be working with Garth.

"I don't like it," Mikkel told him. Worry picked away at his mind, making him feel uneasy. "Bree shouldn't be wandering around these woods alone. What if she falls into something and gets hurt? What if she finds a wild animal?"

When Garth grinned, Mikkel stopped talking. But still—

"I'll tell Nola to help Bree," Garth said. "If she's looking for berries, it's early. But with two of them, they can keep an eye on each other and have a good time talking."

This watching Bree from a distance was going to get them all in trouble. Mikkel felt sure of it. But to his surprise, Bree and Nola brought back long pieces of spruce root they could use in building.

Late in the day everyone gathered for their evening meal. They were in the midst of eating when suddenly Leif leaped up. "A sail!" he exclaimed.

When the others looked out across the bay to the waters of Straumfjord, most of them couldn't see what Leif was talking about.

"It's still far off," he said, "but on this side of Current Island! It must be Thorstein!"

With a bound Mikkel headed for the ship, lowered

Leif's banner, and attached it to a long narrow pole. Then he set off running.

Across the grassy area with scattered trees he ran. Between the alder, birch, and fir at the base of the rocky ridge he ran. Then up the steep side of the ridge. When he reached the top, he ran to the end of the headland. There he stood, waving Leif's banner.

But Thorstein didn't need Mikkel's help. As Leif had expected, Thorstein sailed straight toward them. He, too, had climbed the steep rocky island from which Leif looked around. Thorstein had also studied the area for markers and a favorable site. And there at Straumfjord, Current Fjord, Thorstein found the bay where Leif had started building his camp.

Leif grinned. Though he had never seemed to worry about his brother, relief filled his voice. But it was more. "You didn't know exactly where we'd be, but you found us!" he told Thorstein. "When needed, other people will find us too. We'll offer a gateway for people entering or leaving this new world."

With the additional men from Thorstein's crew, the work moved forward quickly. Leif had spaced the three houses about a hundred feet apart along the narrow terrace. Each house had a large hall and a workshop, as well as a smaller, one-room hut nearby.

Leif's house was the farthest north, Thorstein's house was the farthest south, and in between was the house for the men hired as crew. With a length of about eighty-seven feet, Thorstein's house was double the size of Erik the Red's house in Greenland.

Leif's house was even larger with a little over two thousand square feet of floor space. While the houses for Leif and Thorstein had many rooms, the house between theirs was smaller with a large eating and sleeping room, a carpentry shop, and a storage room.

The long sod walls for Leif's house were the first to be completed. To support the inner walls and the roof, the men set upright fir poles inside the rows of turf. But all the time they worked, both Mikkel and Garth still watched. Neither of them wanted Hammer to lose his opportunity to live.

On a sunny morning Mikkel started shaping the wood for the panels on the inside walls of Leif's house. Long ago he had become a skillful carpenter. By now Mikkel felt proud of whatever he built. Yet no matter how hard he worked, he couldn't push aside his uneasy feelings.

Mikkel's promise to watch Bree from a distance still upset him. Yet he understood the reasons for Devin's request.

Already Mikkel had stayed in Greenland for three years instead of keeping his promise to set Bree free after one voyage. How many times had he said, "This is still one voyage"? How could Devin ever respect him if he didn't keep another promise?

When Shadow came over, wagging his tail for attention, Mikkel was glad to put aside his ax. Once the dog had a good Norwegian name, but not even Mikkel remembered it anymore. Kneeling down, he held Shadow's head between his hands and spoke as if the dog could understand every word.

"Bree called you Shadow because you follow her around. But you take care of her, hear?"

Instantly Shadow pricked his ears as if listening. Mikkel looked around, hoping no one could hear. Tell a dog to take care of Bree? Someone who wanted her independence more than anyone else on earth?

Just the same, Mikkel spoke to Shadow again. "Take care of Bree in all the ways Dev and I can't."

When Shadow cocked his head and woofed, Mikkel felt even more foolish. Ask a dog who was often disobedient for help?

Then Mikkel remembered. In the most important choice he had ever made, he had come to God when lost in a fog off Greenland. After three days of not being able to see where he was, Mikkel felt desperate. He knew how much he needed help.

Now Mikkel felt that need again. Bree had told him that the Christian God could be with him wherever he was. If that was true, He could also be with Bree every moment of the day and night. Just the same, Mikkel added a prayer. "Will You help me be in the right place at the right time?"

When Mikkel picked up his ax again, he went back to making panels. The next time he looked up, he saw Garth standing near Leif's house, supervising the men. Mikkel could see the worry in Garth's face.

Because of his great strength, Hammer was one of the men lifting the long ridgepole. Setting it in place at the peak of the high roof was heavy and dangerous.

As Mikkel watched, he felt the tension deep in his bones. One wrong move and the log would crash down on every man below. At the very least they would be seriously injured. More likely, they would lose their lives under the crushing weight.

And Hammer? Even if it wasn't his fault, he would be blamed.

NINE

THE DARK SECRET

For some time Bree had been watching the blueberries that grew in the bog behind the houses. When they were ready to eat, she picked up a bucket and headed for the nearest bush.

She found the branches heavy with fruit. As soon as Bree tasted the berries, she wanted more. Eating as fast as she picked, she made her way from one low bush to the next. Then she decided that as a cook she better save a few for someone else.

The biggest berries grew on the side of the stream. More than once, Bree slipped on the edge of the bank, almost tumbling into the water. By the time she returned to the cooking fire, she felt proud of herself. Her large bucket was full to the brim.

Her brother Devin was talking to Hammer, and she held out the berries for them to see. But Devin started laughing.

"What's the matter?" Bree asked.

"You're as dirty as if you were a little girl."

Bree looked down at her long dress and flushed. Most of the time she loved Devin, but sometimes his memory was too good. If she wasn't careful, he would tell about the time when—

But Hammer surprised her. "Maybe there's a reason why Bree is so dirty."

Strange. Hammer wasn't teasing. And his eyes didn't hold his usual anger.

Instead, Hammer looked excited. "Show me where you picked berries," he said.

Bree led the two of them back to the grassy bank along the stream. It was easy to see where she had been. Not only were the branches of the blueberry bushes bare —more than once she had slipped in the soft bank, leaving holes of black dirt.

Kneeling down, Hammer dug with his hands, bringing up reddish lumps of earth. "I thought so," he said.

One of the pieces was as big as a fist. When he broke open the clump, the dirt looked black and reddish orange. As he turned it toward the sun, small bits of soil reflected light.

"What is it?" Bree asked.

"Bog ore." For the first time since Bree met him, Hammer's voice was filled with satisfaction. "We can make nails from this."

When Devin told Leif what Hammer had found, the leader hurried over. With one look at the bog ore, he made his decision.

"You just earned your right to stop cutting turf and peeling bark," he told Hammer. "Devin is a good blacksmith, but I want you to teach him how to extract bog ore. And you're in charge of building the furnace hut."

As Leif walked away, Hammer stood there watching him go, as if he couldn't believe what had happened. When he turned back to Bree and Devin, Hammer looked like a different person.

First he picked out a site for a sod hut on the other side of the stream. Close to water and separate from the houses in case of fire, the location was just what Hammer wanted for a furnace.

A short distance away, he and Devin dug a pit for a kiln. There they could light fresh wood, cover it with sod, and leave it to smolder and become charcoal. Then they searched for a large flat stone they could use for an anvil. By the end of the afternoon Hammer and Devin had carried logs for building the sod hut across the stream.

When everyone gathered for their late-day meal they already knew what had happened. Hammer had found a rich source of bog ore. In spite of the way all of them felt about Hammer, they were grateful. Both Thorstein and Leif had brought along extra rivets and nails. Yet both ships had faced stormy seas. The nails Hammer produced with the bog ore could make the difference in whether they reached home safely or not.

The next morning Hammer showed Devin how to collect clumps of reddish black ore from the boggy ground next to the terrace. In the places where men cut turf for the houses, it was easy to see veins of ore.

Then Hammer and Devin started work on the furnace hut. Set into a bank of earth that gave shelter from the wind, the front side of the sod hut was open to the stream.

Whenever possible, Bree slipped across the stream to talk with Devin. One day Hammer sat down for a moment and she asked, "What did Mikkel do to you?"

Bree meant to say, "Why did you start hating Mikkel a long time ago?" Instead Hammer talked about the day in the forest when he and Mikkel chopped down one tree after another. He described how the wind had come up.

"Mikkel stopped working," Hammer told them. "He wouldn't drop another tree. He said, 'I don't want to take a chance on hurting you.'"

Hammer's laugh was hard with scorn. "How can he think I'm dumb enough to believe that!" The resentment was back in his eyes. "I want to keep hating Mikkel."

When Bree and Devin fell silent, Hammer looked at Bree. "Aren't you mad at Mikkel?"

"Sometimes he makes me really angry," she said. "He took me from my family and everything I love. It used to be worse because I was scared of sailing, scared of the dragon head, scared of everything."

"But don't you hate him?" Hammer asked.

Bree shook her head. "Not anymore."

When did it change? she wondered. Now she was more afraid that Mikkel would disappoint her again—that he wouldn't keep his promise to set her free.

"Bree is doing better," Devin said.

"Why?" Hammer's question hung in the air between them.

Bree thought about it. "I guess it's because I kept forgiving him—"

"Once?"

"Over and over again." Bree still felt a jerk in her heart, just remembering how hard it had been, getting used to being a slave. "I can't count how many times."

"Hammer, what did Mikkel do to hurt you?" Devin asked. "To make you angry a long time ago?"

Suddenly Hammer stood up. "Leif says I'm supposed to work with you. He didn't say I have to answer your questions." When Hammer stalked away, even his shoulders looked angry.

"How can he do it?" Bree whispered when he was far

enough away. "Even when he's upset, Hammer moves as silently as a cat. It scares me."

Devin agreed. "He's so big and strong, but he doesn't make a sound. And no matter what I do, he doesn't want to talk. About what really happened, I mean."

"But did you hear what Hammer said? Mikkel has changed."

Devin shrugged.

"Really. Mikkel has changed. Aren't you glad? I want to respect him."

"So do I, and often I do. But still—"

"The secret," Bree said.

Devin nodded. "Mikkel's dark secret."

Not only had he led a raid on the monastery near their home. All of Mikkel's family, friends, and neighbors knew about that. But he had also stolen coins from Bjorn the cobbler, his father's best friend in Dublin. Only three people knew about that.

Bjorn, Devin, and Bree.

For three and a half years Bree had searched for Mikkel's hiding place. Then, just before leaving Greenland, she discovered it. Now she knew how to find the treasure again.

In the worst possible moment Mikkel learned that Bree had found his horde. A leather bag of coins he had earned. A bag of precious gems he had taken from the monastery. And the bag that offered the biggest problem of all. Because of the cobbler's mark in the leather Bree could identify which bag of coins belonged to Bjorn. But Mikkel didn't know that she knew.

Whenever Bree thought about Mikkel's horde she saw the stolen coins and gems as evidence of Mikkel's greed. "That wooden keg holds what you think is wealth," she spit out when she was really upset. "But it can hurt you more than anything you know."

"I'll take care of the treasure," Mikkel answered.

"And how will you take care of it?"

"It's not your worry."

"Not my worry?" Bree's anger had spilled out of control. It was the Irish he had robbed. Her people. And it was Mikkel's honesty that was involved. If he didn't set things right, it would ruin his life.

"I'm just glad that Mikkel doesn't know all that I know," she told Devin. Strangely, their father, Aidan, was also a friend of Bjorn's and traded with the cobbler in Dublin.

"Just make sure you don't ever let on about Bjorn," Devin warned Bree as he had countless times before. "Mikkel has come a long way. But if he knows what we know, we might never get back to Ireland."

Bree sighed. Each time she started to believe that Mikkel had really changed, his dark secret came up. "Will Mikkel ever get over his love of fame and money? Will we ever be able to completely trust him?"

As Bree headed back across the stream, Devin called after her. "When you get home, Tully will be waiting."

Suddenly Bree felt better. She turned back. "You think so, Dev?"

"I'm sure of it."

He was still the big brother. Dev was telling her to protect her heart.

TEN

WHO IS TULLY?

To Bree's relief Mikkel stayed out of her way. If he did as Leif asked and watched out for her, she didn't know about it. She only noticed that Mikkel seemed to be running a lot. If that was his way of making sure she was all right, fair enough. He wasn't interfering with her freedom.

From the place on the terrace where she and Nola prepared food, Bree often saw what Devin and Hammer were doing. After finishing the sod hut, Hammer built the furnace. First he dug a shallow pit. Next he made a small frame by setting stones over the pit. Using clay, he sealed the stones together into an airtight chamber.

As soon as he was ready to produce iron, Hammer

roasted the bog ore by putting lumps of ore on top of wood to burn off the water. Then he packed the furnace, alternating layers of ore with layers of charcoal. The extremely hot temperature produced by charcoal made the ore fluid. Though the separation wasn't perfect, the iron dropped to the bottom of the pit and impurities collected as slag around it.

When the firing was done, Hammer smashed open the stone furnace. The iron in the pit looked like a sponge—a big porous rock with ridges, shiny lumps, bits of clay, and unburned charcoal. After reheating the sponge, Hammer pounded it into a bloom at a high temperature to get out still more impurities.

At last Hammer said the iron was ready to be forged. From that point on, Devin had enough experience as a blacksmith to know what to do.

After setting in place the ridgepole for Leif's house, men used pole after pole for rafters—the slanted beams that supported the high roof. When the rafters were ready, men wove countless branches between them to make the base for the sod roof. After laying the turf, they stretched spruce-root cords over the top of the roof. Weighted with stones at both ends, the cords held down the sod and protected it from winds off the sea.

Leif's house was very large with six rooms that included three living and sleeping rooms in a row. The small private room at the end was for Leif. The other two were bigger, and all three had a fireplace in the middle of the floor. The house also had a kitchen with a stone oven and two storage rooms. A lean-to at one side of the house was large enough to build or repair a small boat.

On the early August day that men laid the long stone hearth in the central living and sleeping room, Mikkel was still paneling the inside walls. Along those walls, other men built the benches that were used for sitting and sleeping. When they finished their work, Bree, Nola, and Hekja spread grasses on the dirt floor.

Tyrker the German helped them move their cooking pots inside. A house slave, Tyrker had taken care of Leif when he was a child. Though short in height, he was strong and athletic and known for his ability in sports.

Each morning Bree and Nola walked from where they stayed on the ship to prepare meals in the house. Besides the hearth, there was a cooking pit for roasting food and a pit lined with stones for storing embers at night. Long chains hung down from the ceiling to hold cooking pots over the fire.

After being outside much of the summer Bree found it hard to get used to the dark room lit only by the fire and hollowed-out stones used as oil lamps. Whenever possible she opened the smoke holes and the door.

Mikkel was one of those who moved into Leif's house and took his meals there. Though careful to look polite, Bree ignored him every way she could. Whenever she dished up soup or porridge she looked at his bowl instead of him. Then she realized that Mikkel was also avoiding her. At first she felt relieved. Then she wondered about it.

When most of the work was finished on the house for Thorstein and the center dwelling for men in the ship crews, Garth built a small house for himself and Nola. At one end he partitioned off a room for Bree that doubled as a weaving place during the day. As with the other houses, Garth's had a dirt floor that Bree and Nola covered with grasses.

Haki and Hekja, the Scottish slaves, were the last to move off the ship. Their round hut was next to Garth's house and closest to the stream.

When heather and wildflowers filled the grassy areas, Bree decided that Leif's house needed something more. As she dug up flowers, she took only part of a clump and left the rest to grow. She was still planting gold and white flowers next to the door when Leif and Mikkel returned.

Leif stopped and spoke to her. "Thanks, Bree. You're making this look like a home instead of a camp."

When Leif went inside, Mikkel surprised Bree by dropping down on a large stump left by the workers. For days at a time they had not talked with each other. Now he told her, "Wherever you are, you make a home."

Her back turned to him, Bree kept working. From her earliest memory her mother had taught her to take whatever they had and use it to give beauty and comfort. Since becoming a slave, Bree hadn't realized that such a simple act as planting flowers was part of being the person she was.

As she planted and watered the last flower, she forgot herself and spoke in the Irish.

"God bless this house," Mikkel said softly.

Bree whirled around. It surprised her that Mikkel understood her words. Since her capture they had spoken Norse, a trade language Bree and Devin learned from their father. "How did you know?" she asked Mikkel.

"From listening to you Irish. But I don't know why you say it."

Remembering the customs of her people always made Bree long for home. When she spoke again the sound of her voice held her love for the green fields and misty mountains.

"When an Irishman finishes building a house and turns it over to the owner, he blesses it. Now I've finished my work. The flowers are ready to grow, so I say, 'God bless this house.' And when Nola sees what I've done, she'll tell me, 'God bless your work.'"

"I'll say it for Nola," Mikkel told her. "God bless your work, Briana."

Again Bree felt the surprise of his words. These days she seldom heard her real name. In that moment she realized how important it was to her.

As she gathered up her tools, Mikkel spoke again. "Dev said I should ask you something."

"He did?" It didn't seem like her brother. "So what big joke is he playing?"

But Mikkel was serious. "Bree, who is Tully?"

Bree stared at him. Though Mikkel had asked her before, she had never explained. It hurt too much.

At first she could not answer. She could only wonder if Mikkel heard the pounding of her heart. Why didn't Dev tell him what needed to be said? He must have had a special reason.

Now, four years away from what had happened, Bree still struggled to speak. "He's the lad I thought I saw when I saw you."

"The lad you *thought* you saw?"

"I was coming down from my favorite place in the mountains when I looked toward the stepping-stones. When my brother Adam and younger sisters swam in a safe place upstream I took care of them. The river was high from recent rains, and Daddy had often warned me about a swift place in the river."

Bree stopped, swallowed hard, and went on. "I knew that just below the stones, the river narrowed, and the current was especially swift. I saw you and thought it was Tully—"

"I look like him?"

"From the back. Your hair is the same. The way you stand. Then you started to cross the river."

"I fell and hit my head."

To Bree the memory of that moment still seemed a nightmare. A strong swimmer, she had always watched out for younger children when they swam. Being sure that someone was safe was important to her. And Tully? From earliest memory he had been Devin's friend and then hers also.

"You didn't want Tully to drown," Mikkel said when Bree could not speak. For an instant she caught a glimpse of understanding in his eyes. Then he looked away.

On that clear day the steep, rocky sides of Current Island rose high in the distance. But Mikkel seemed to see far beyond.

When he faced Bree again he said, "Because you kept me from drowning I was able to lead the raid."

Still too upset to speak, Bree nodded. As though it had happened only yesterday, the grief of it filled her heart.

"And you want to marry Tully."

It was not a question, and this time Bree could answer. "If he'll have me."

"How do you know he'll wait for you?"

For Bree that was the most unkind question of all. "I don't," she said. "And how can I expect him to wait when he doesn't know if I'm alive? If I'll ever come home?"

Wanting only to get away, she jumped up, leaving her tools. When she started running, she hardly knew what she was doing. Her sight blurred by tears, she headed for the bay, but then kept going.

Between the bushes and trees, then up the steep slope she ran. To the top of the rocky ridge she ran. Reaching the other side, she dropped down on a large boulder, covered her face with her hands, and sobbed her heart out.

When at last she drew a long shuddering breath, Mikkel spoke from behind her. "I'm sorry."

"Sorry?" Bree spit out the word. "Sorry for four lost years?"

When he dropped down beside her, Bree looked up, embarrassed to have him see her face. Swollen it would be, red from tears. Bree turned away, wanting to hide her face and her grief.

But Mikkel spoke to her back.

"I ask your forgiveness."

When she didn't answer he spoke again. "I will take you home."

"Home?" Angry now, Bree whirled on him. "Three years ago you made Dev and me a promise. 'Go with me for one voyage,' you told him. 'When we return to Aurland I'll set your sister free.'

"'Free' you said! Remember? For three long years you stayed in Greenland. 'This is still one voyage,' you said, every time we asked to go home. Don't you dare make me another empty promise. Don't you dare say you will set me free unless you mean it!"

Unwilling to even look at him, Bree covered her face with her hands.

When the silence stretched long between them, Bree dropped her hands and looked once more into his eyes. What she saw there frightened her. Only once before had she seen such pain. In that moment Mikkel talked of his oldest brother—the brother who had been his closest friend. But that brother had died at sea.

Now, as Mikkel spoke to Bree, the pain both of them felt stood like a wall between them. "On the day we set foot in this new world, I asked if we could start over," he said. "I promised that you would be able to trust me. And I promise you again. When we leave here, I will take you to Ireland—straight home instead of going to Norway first. And I will set you free."

Bree stared at him. As she looked into his face she hardly dared to breathe. Did Mikkel really mean what he was saying?

ELEVEN

THE WILD RIDE

For some time Leif and his men had been eager to explore the long waterway they had first seen from Current Island. Because of its swift and dangerous currents they called that channel Straumfjord or Current Fjord. In mid-August Leif left Thorstein and his crew to finish the work that had to be done before winter.

Standing near the stern of Leif's ship, Bree felt surprised at how glad she was to be on the water again. At first she had been afraid to sail. Now she realized that a love of sailing had crept up on her. What new places would they see?

I want to go home, she told herself as she had a hundred times before. *I want to be in Ireland. Still—*

Bree didn't want to finish the thought. How could she possibly feel torn between wanting to be with the people she loved and liking what she was doing now? But Devin seemed just as eager to explore this new world.

Before long, they saw flocks of puffins. With fast wing beats they flew straight and low over the surface of the water. Sometimes there were dozens of these birds. At other times there were hundreds. With a big head and stocky body, they had a black cap, neck, and back, and a white underside. Their webbed feet and heavy-looking triangular bills were orange.

As Bree watched, the puffins swooped down, landed on the water, and dove beneath the surface. Using both feet and wings, they seemed to fly underwater. When they came back up, their beaks were filled with small fish.

Soon Leif's ship passed nesting islands where puffins had made deep burrows in the grassy slopes of low cliffs. Adult puffins flew back and forth, bringing fish to their chicks.

Farther on, a long range of flat-topped mountains rose high above the fjord. Bree wished she could leave the ship and see more. The highest peak looked round and bald, and she loved climbing to high places. The sight of those mountains made her lonesome for home.

During the voyage Bree celebrated her seventeenth birthday. To her surprise Mikkel was the first to offer good wishes for her new year. Devin was next, and then

Nola. As they cooked the early day meal, Nola held out a gift—two woven headbands of red wool.

Bree gasped. "*Red* headbands?" A slave wore clothing of undyed wool and Bree often longed for color.

Bree could hardly believe it. She could never figure out how Nola managed so much. Even when newly captured she had found a way to take care of the younger girls.

"You're giving me something red?" Bree asked.

Nola's quiet smile was Bree's only answer.

"And *two* of them?" Running her hand across the headbands, Bree felt the beautiful bright color in her heart.

With great care she tucked one of the headbands into the sea chest Mikkel's mother had given her. Countless times Bree had been grateful for the watertight chest that kept her food and clothing dry. Now Bree used the other headband to pull back her long wavy hair.

Leaning close, Nola whispered in her ear. "Whenever you wear one of them, remember that you're still a chieftain's daughter."

Tears welled up in Bree's eyes. Blinking, she swallowed hard before she could speak. "And he and Mam love me very much."

By now they had sailed far down Current Fjord, a long distance beyond the land that Haki and Hekja had run across in order to give a report to Leif. Soon after the early day meal, Bree caught sight of smoke rising above the trees. Then she saw a mother and four children gathering shells along the shore.

As the ship drew closer, the mother looked up and immediately spoke to the children. Instantly they disappeared into the trees with the woman close behind.

"Oh! We frightened them!" Bree felt sorry and thought she understood. As though it were yesterday, she remembered the first time she saw the great snarling dragon at the bow of Mikkel's ship. Whenever possible, she had turned her back to that dragon, not wanting to look.

Later on they sailed into warmer waters where huge herds of walrus and seals sunned themselves on the shore. Geese, ducks, and birds that Bree didn't recognize flew up from their nests in sheltered coves.

When Leif turned the tiller over to Mikkel he stood straight and tall with pride in every part of his being. As the wind picked up, it blew Mikkel's hair around his sun-bronzed face.

Though Leif's ship was much larger and more difficult to handle than his own, it was easy to see that Mikkel loved what he was doing. Alert and careful, he watched for anything that could endanger the ship. Now and then he lifted his head, as though remembering why he liked being at sea.

When they sailed into a large bay the brisk wind still filled the red-and-white sail. At Leif's direction, Mikkel turned the ship toward land and the mouth of a river. They were still a long way from shore when Bree felt a thud.

Suddenly the ship stopped. Men staggered. Bree fell to the deck.

Quickly she picked herself up, and the men around her caught their balance. Everyone spoke at once. Shallow water? Here?

Mikkel groaned, clearly feeling it was his fault. But there could be no doubt about it. The ship had gone aground.

When men put out the small boat they towed, Leif found long sandbars between the ship and the shore. With the tide partly out, those sandbars were hidden by water. As the tide continued to recede, Leif and the men disappeared up the river. Before long, the bay was filled with long stretches of dry land and pools of water caught behind the sandbars.

As the tide flowed back in, water surrounded the ship and lifted it off the sandbar. By the time Leif returned, the water was deep. Taking their places at the oars, men rowed the ship closer to shore.

"This land shall have a name in keeping with its nature," Leif said, as he looked out over the bay. "I call this area Hóp."

The word sounded like Hope, but Mikkel told Devin that the name meant tidal lagoons. Whenever the tide ebbed out, it left shallow pools of water separated by sandbars from the sea.

Now the men used the high tide to continue up the river before letting down the anchor. Once again, as on their first day at Leif's Camp, men stood on the banks of the river catching salmon.

"A river of fish!" Bree exclaimed. "Not a river of water, but of fish!"

Though the men wanted to set up tents on shore, Leif was cautious. "Tonight we'll stay on board ship," he said. "Until we know what we're facing we'll keep together."

Working quickly, the men lowered the sail onto the posts at the center of the ship and drew the cloth out over the sides.

Soon after dark, Bree spread out her sleeping sack between Devin and Nola. The sea air and wind had made her sleepy, but Bree tossed and turned. From her place near the edge of the sail that covered them like a tent, she looked up at the stars.

For a long time she lay awake, listening to the snorts, dips, and mountains of someone snoring. Hours later, Bree woke to a flickering light.

Her heart jumped. *What is it?*

Hardly daring to move, she lay there, wondering. Lightning? But that didn't seem right.

Rising up on her elbow, Bree saw the light again. A cooking fire? But the light seemed to move, becoming brighter, then dimming as though farther away.

Quietly Bree crawled out of the covered area under the sail. When she stood up to look over the side of the ship she saw a torch held by a man in a nearby boat. In the light of that torch the boat seemed to be made of skin stretched across a wood frame.

A skin canoe? That day Leif's men had seen one dart off into a small stream.

Now one man sat in the stern of the canoe and paddled. The man holding the torch stood in the bow, looking down into the water.

On hands and knees, Bree crawled back under the sail to shake her brother's shoulder. "Dev!" she whispered. "Wake up!"

By the time Devin joined her, Bree's eyes had grown used to the darkness. Leif's ship was high enough for them to be able to see all that happened.

The harpoon in the man's hand looked like a long spear with a rope attached to it. Without making a sound Bree and Devin watched. Soon they noticed ripples in the water alongside the skin boat. In the light of the torch Bree saw the flip of a tail fin. When she gasped at its size, Devin laid a hand on her arm, warning her.

Seeming to be attracted to the light, the fish swam around the canoe. Now and then Bree saw a part of its head, then a flash of its body. But the man standing at the bow kept waiting. Then, as though the fish had changed direction, the ripples appeared closer to the boat.

Suddenly the man threw the harpoon. The long rope snaked out, snapped tight. In the next instant the man at the bow sat down, braced his feet, and hung on. The boat shot forward in a wild ride.

As the fish fought to get away, the canoe twisted and turned. One moment the line was tight. The next it fell slack. Each time the fish changed direction the canoe tipped one way or another. Again and again the sides dipped close to the water.

When the canoe nearly capsized, Bree gasped again. But the man at the stern stretched out his paddle and set it right.

Moments later, as suddenly as it began, the fight was over. As the men pulled the fish close to their canoe, Bree saw both the head and the tail.

"Whoooh!" Devin exclaimed. "Look at the size of that fish!"

By now, others on Leif's ship had gathered wherever they could in order to see. While the man at the bow of the canoe held the fish steady, the other started paddling again. Together they towed the fish to land, leaped out, and pulled it up on shore.

In the first rays of the rising sun, Bree saw the entire length of the fish. No wonder the men didn't try to pull it on board!

In the next moment Leif and Mikkel vaulted over the side of the ship and headed that way. As the rest of the men followed, Bree and Devin joined them. Before long, every person who could get close enough to see surrounded the two fishermen.

"Leif calls it a sturgeon," Mikkel told Bree and Devin. "Can you believe it?"

The back of the sturgeon was covered with bony plates, but the harpoon still pierced the small soft scales on its stomach.

As they watched, Leif walked over to the canoe. Standing at the bow, he held up his hand. Next he walked to the other end of the canoe and held up his other hand. Then, as though measuring the length of the canoe, he held up both hands and pointed to the fish.

When the two fishermen grinned, the men from Leif's ship looked just as excited. Bree felt sure that for years to come this would be the greatest fish story ever told, whether by the men who caught it, the Norwegians, Greenlanders, or Irish.

It was a good beginning. As the two men cleaned the sturgeon, they answered Leif's questions. Using many signs between them, they tried to understand each other. When they finished talking, Leif explained to the men on his ship.

Leif believed that the fishermen knew a wide range of land—that their people lived in different areas according to the seasons and what berries and game would be available to them.

Later that morning Leif sent out the Scottish runners again. "Come back in three days and tell me what you see," Leif told Haki and Hekja.

Planning to explore farther than the day before, Leif

also took Mikkel and other young men up the river in the small boat. When they returned they were excited about the many kinds of trees they had found. Oaks and maples, cedars and spruce! Trees tall enough to make masts for the biggest ships! And at high tide the water would be deep enough to take the ship still farther upstream.

When the incoming tide washed into the mouth of the river, they moved the ship again. On the edge of a quiet pond the men set up tents. Quickly they fit together wood braces, then stretched large pieces of wool cloth over the frame.

Leif and Garth set out, marking the trees they wanted to take. As Mikkel and Hammer dropped them, other men trimmed off the branches and started peeling the bark. In Greenland, trees were in such short supply that their load of timber would be very valuable.

Carrying the buckets she needed, Bree walked a short distance upstream to get water. As she followed the shore of the river, she had the strange feeling that she was not alone. Stopping suddenly, she looked around, but saw nothing.

At an opening between trees, she waded into the water. A small island covered with trees lay in the middle of the river. Here, close to shore, the water was shallow. Bree waited for the sand to settle and then filled her buckets. When she looked up, Bree was sure that she saw a shadow between the trees. Moments later it was gone.

As she started back to the ship, Bree again felt sure that someone was watching. This time Bree whirled around.

TWELVE

WHERE'S TYRKER?

I nstantly a young girl stepped behind a tree. Slowly, staying out in the open so she wouldn't frighten her, Bree walked back in that direction.

When she reached the place where the girl disappeared, Bree stopped again. She felt sure the girl had hidden behind a large oak, but when she didn't appear, Bree sat down on a large stone and waited.

Shafts of sunlight sifted down between the trees. Before long, Bree heard the call of a bird from somewhere nearby. As she turned her head to listen, the call came again. Then, from farther away, the same kind of call answered.

Still Bree waited. Then suddenly and without making

a sound, two children stepped out of the trees. Bree watched them as they watched her.

The boy was younger, perhaps six or seven, Bree thought. His chest was bare, and he wore leggings and soft leather shoes. The girl was taller and three or four years older. Her long black hair shone in the sunlight. A piece of cord around the top of her head held her hair away from her face.

Hoping she wouldn't frighten them away, Bree stood up slowly. Pointing to herself she said, "Bree."

The girl's eyes sparkled when she smiled. "Nikmaq," she said.

Bree repeated it. "Nikmaq." The girl nodded and smiled again.

The boy seemed to have no fear. Pointing to Bree's buckets, he motioned for her to pick them up. Then he ran a short distance, stopped, and waited. Each time Bree and Nikmaq followed, he raced ahead again. Twice more he stopped and waited for them to catch up. At last he came to a large tree and climbed rapidly upward.

As he crawled out on one of the limbs, his sister stepped back. Moments later, the boy shook the branch, and nuts fell to the ground.

Looking at Bree, the girl smiled, pointed to the nuts, then to Bree.

"For me?" Bree pointed to herself.

Taking a bucket, the girl emptied the water and started filling it with nuts. From one spreading branch to another the boy climbed. Each time he shook a limb, more nuts rained down on the ground. Bree and the girl scurried to pick them up.

Before long the buckets could hold no more, and the boy climbed down and disappeared. But the girl picked up a flat rock, used a much larger rock as a table, and showed Bree how to crack the nut open.

When the inner part fell out Bree wasn't sure what to do. In Ireland she was used to hazelnuts, but whatever this was, it was larger.

Again the girl helped her out. Picking up the pieces, she ate them, smiled, and then pointed to Bree.

The moment Bree tasted the inner part of the butternut, she also smiled. It was good, and best of all, it wasn't cod.

That evening, as they gathered around the late-day meal, Leif stopped in the midst of eating and asked, "Where's Tyrker?"

Known as Tyrker the German or Tyrker the Southerner, the household slave had often helped Bree and Nola.

"I saw him after we finished chopping down trees," Garth said. "He was headed that way."

Garth pointed upstream. "But I didn't see him after that."

No one had seen him after that.

Worry filled Leif's eyes. "I told you to stay close to the ship, to go two by two or in groups. Who was with my foster-father today?"

As Leif looked around the circle no one spoke. But then Leif remembered. "It was you, Hammer. What have you to say for yourself?"

"We started out together. Something caught Tyrker's attention, and suddenly he left the path we knew."

"You didn't go after him?"

"I tried, but I couldn't find him. The undergrowth is thick, and—"

Hammer stopped, swallowed hard. "He's so skilled in everything he does, I was sure he'd know his way back."

"That's no excuse," Leif said. "When I was a child, Tyrker took care of me. He was as good and kind as a mother. I want no harm to come to him."

Angry now, Leif stared at Hammer until the man's gaze met his. "Are you telling me everything?"

Fear leaped into Hammer's eyes. "I swear it."

But Leif would not let him off. "We have shown mercy to you. Have you shown mercy to him?"

"No harm has come to Tyrker at my hand."

Leif's strong gaze searched the man's face until

Hammer seemed unable to bear it. When he looked at the ground, Leif pushed aside his food and stood up.

"This should not have happened. No one was to be separated from the ship or another person. Hammer, if Tyrker is harmed, I will hold you personally responsible."

Leif looked around the group. "I want twelve men— you included, Hammer. Take us to where you saw Tyrker last. For your sake, as well as his, I hope we find him in good health."

Each man already carried a knife in its sheath. Taking up their swords, spears, bows, and arrows, they set out with Leif.

As they left the clearing, Bree saw Hammer's eyes. He was angry again. But there was more. Hammer was as frightened as he had been the night the men decided his fate. If Tyrker the German was truly gone—lost, dead, never to be found—there would be no mercy.

From her mother Bree had learned how to care for injured people. Now she prepared for the worst. Quickly she added wood to the fire, then hung a pot of water to heat. If they found Tyrker, if he was hurt—

As a house slave, the man Leif called a foster-father was responsible for indoor tasks, such as taking care of children. From the first day of the expedition he had helped Bree, quietly teaching her what she did not know.

Could he have fallen? Lost his way? Short and frail

looking, he had dark wrinkles in his face. A master of all kinds of crafts, he had always been kind to Bree. Now she felt upset, not only for Leif's sake, but even more, for Tyrker.

Soon night would be upon them. In some places the trees stretched tall, reaching for the sun. In other places the tangled undergrowth might make it impossible for them to find him.

The water had barely started to heat when Bree heard a shout. As she ran that direction, Devin and the remaining men followed.

As he stood in front of Leif, Tyrker seemed even shorter than usual. Leif's face was filled with relief as he asked, "Why are you so late returning, foster-father?"

In his excitement, Tyrker's eyes darted in all directions. When he tried to speak, Bree couldn't understand his words. Even Leif seemed to have trouble with them.

"Tyrker," he said. "Tell us, please, what happened."

But Tyrker was still too excited to explain. Resting his hand on Tyrker's shoulder, Leif looked directly into his eyes. "Foster-father—"

As Leif spoke in Norse, Tyrker grew more calm. Then he, too, spoke in the Norse language.

"I had gone only a bit farther than Hammer and the rest of you," he explained. "But I have news to tell you. I found grapevines and grapes."

Leif stared at him. "Are you sure of this, foster-father? *Really* sure?"

"I am absolutely sure. Where I was born, there was no lack of grapevines and grapes."

Around them the forest had grown dark, but it wasn't hard to hear that Leif was also excited. Not only was he grateful to find the man he had loved since childhood. Tyrker's news was astonishing!

If it's really true, it's like finding gold, Bree thought. In northern countries it was too cold to grow grapes. This discovery might offer an unending supply.

But when everyone returned to the clearing next to the ship, Bree saw the look in Hammer's face. Sitting apart from the other men, he turned his back to the group.

Soon Garth stood up and walked over. As Hammer shook his head, his twin brother walked away.

When Devin tried to talk with Hammer, he again shook his head. Then Mikkel went over and dropped down on the grass. Like Hammer, he sat with his back to the group. For a long time Mikkel waited there without speaking.

Finally he started talking. Though Hammer didn't look at Mikkel, he seemed to listen.

Leaning forward, Bree strained to hear what Mikkel said. But not a word reached her ears.

The next morning Bree had the early day meal ready

before the sun rose. *Porridge again,* she thought. *Even in this land of abundance, we eat porridge.*

But then Bree decided that she didn't mind. When she made porridge the men ate quickly, taking no thought for what she served them. The moment they finished eating, she would follow them to see the grapes.

As they left camp, Tyrker marched like the leader of a conquering army. Walking beside him, Leif towered over the smaller man. This morning Leif looked even more excited. And from the top of his head to the end of his smallest toes, Tyrker looked proud.

When they reached the place he had found, Tyrker stretched out his hand, as though introducing a large tree to the company of men.

At first Leif stood back, as if wondering where he should look. Then he saw it. Vines had grown up the tree, winding their way around the trunk. From those vines hung heavy clusters of grapes.

Leif shouted his laughter. Then he pounded Tyrker's back. Then he stood aside for all to see. And when Bree and Nola and every man among them had a chance to look, Leif took his knife from its sheath.

Handing it to Tyrker he said, "To you I give the honor of cutting the first grapes."

Bending low, Tyrker bowed to Leif. When he straightened again, Tyrker's eyes were wet. Carefully he cut the first cluster from the vine. Even more carefully he handed it to Leif and bowed again.

"I name this land Vinland for its natural qualities," Leif said.

On the evening of the third day Haki and Hekja returned. As before, when they told about the land surrounding Leif's Camp, they gave another good report. In addition to the herds of walrus and seals already seen, black bear, moose, caribou, and birds of all kinds were abundant. Countless bushes offered berries easily picked from the land. And rivers of fish!

Haki and Hekja also brought Leif a sheaf of self-sown wheat—a wild grass that grew in low-lying moist areas. It looked much like Norse wheat.

"A goodly land," Leif said as he received it. More than once Bree saw him look around, as though scarcely able to believe the abundance.

From then on, Leif split the group into two work crews. "We'll divide our time between the two tasks," he said.

In the days that followed, some picked grapes and carried them back until the small after-boat was filled with kegs of grapes and juice. Other men dropped trees, including the vine wood—the valuable oaks and maples around which the vines had wrapped while climbing to the light. Bree was among those who picked grapes, and one morning the girl she had met earlier appeared again.

"Nikmaq!" Bree exclaimed.

"Nikmaq!" The girl's black eyes flashed as she offered her lovely smile.

This time she had a wooden carrier on her back. Laced inside the carrier was a very young baby wrapped in an animal skin.

Bree pointed to the child. "Brother?"

Nikmaq stared at her, a question in her eyes.

"Brother?" Bree asked again.

Clearly puzzled, Nikmaq knelt down and began drawing in a patch of soft ground. First a large figure, a man with leggings, moccasins, and a shirt with long sleeves. Next to him a smaller figure wearing a skirt. When Nikmaq drew a still smaller figure next to the woman, she pointed to herself.

Then she drew yet another figure that was smaller yet and clearly a boy. Last of all she drew the baby in a wooden carrier.

Bree pointed first to the drawing of the boy and said, "Brother." Then she pointed to the baby, and repeated, "Brother."

"Brother." As Nikmaq smiled, her black eyes flashed with the fun of it. "Brother," she said again, as though she liked the sound of the word.

Taking the carrier off her back, she hung it by a strap

over a low-hanging branch. With a soft tap on the wood she set the carrier swinging, rocking the baby gently. Then she picked up a woven basket and walked over to where the vines were heavy with grapes.

Bree's bucket was full, but she helped her new friend pick one cluster after another. When the basket was full, Nikmaq held it out.

"No, no," Bree tried to explain. "I was just helping."

The girl held it out again. Again Bree tried to say no. But Nikmaq kept offering the large, beautifully woven basket. When Bree tried to tell her she would empty the basket and return it to her, Nikmaq shook her head.

Finally Bree nodded. This time she used her hands to say, "What can I give you?"

Suddenly Nikmaq reached out. With a light touch her fingers stroked the red headband holding back Bree's hair. Instantly Bree pulled it off and handed it to her new friend.

By the time Leif was ready to leave the land of tidal lagoons, Bree had visited Nikmaq's wigwam—a shelter built with poles, then covered with birch bark. Other wigwams were covered with hides, birch bark, reed mats, or a combination of the three.

When hunting, Nikmaq's brother carried a bow he stored inside the skin of a cougar's tail to protect it from getting wet. And the men soaked moose skins in oil before placing them over the frame of a canoe.

Bree also learned another way of cooking by using a "kettle" made from a large hardwood log. With the center burned and the charred part chopped out to make a deep hole, Nikmaq filled the hollow with water. Using wooden tongs, she dropped in hot stones to heat the water and cook their meat.

But it wasn't until the last day in Hóp that Bree discovered she had never called her friend by the right name. As Leif's men loaded the ship with logs, the people of the tidal lagoons began to gather around. Word traveled fast, for one after another they came, often greeting Leif by calling out, "Nikmaq! Nikmaq!" More than once the word sounded like Micmac.

"Nikmaq?" Bree asked Leif. "That's the name of my friend. But it sounds like they're greeting you."

"They are," he told her. "The word means *my kin-friends.*"

"My kin-friend," Bree repeated slowly. "My relative. My family. But also my friend."

Suddenly one of the women spoke to Leif, then pointed to Bree.

Leif looked at the woman, lifted his hands, palms up, as though to say, "What do you mean?"

The woman moved forward, again pointed to Bree, and then to her own head.

Leif grinned. "Sorry, Bree. I think she likes your headband."

Bree gulped. The red headbands from Nola had been her treasured possessions. Whenever she wore one of them Bree remembered that she was the daughter of a chieftain who loved her very much. She had given the first headband willingly to her new friend. This was the only one left.

As Bree took it off, she told herself to smile, and she did. But then as she held it out she hoped the woman would enjoy the color as much as she did.

When the woman accepted the headband, her eyes glowed. In that moment Bree felt better. She would cherish the birch bark basket she received in exchange.

Now everyone pressed forward. One man after another held out an animal skin—either one that he wore or an extra one. Women walking out of the forest brought clay pots or the bladder of a large animal filled with oil. Leif and the other men opened their sea chests and began trading their goods.

But all the while Bree kept watching for her friend, wanting to say good-bye to the girl she knew as Nikmaq. As Leif's crew started to take up the anchor, Bree finally saw her hurry across the shore.

"Wait!" Bree told the men who were ready to leave. Giving them no chance to say no, Bree ran down the ramp. She did not stop until she stood in front of her friend.

"Nikmaq," Bree said softly. "My kin-friend. My family. My friend."

"Nikmaq," the girl replied. Then she practiced the new words. "My kin-friend. My family. My friend."

THIRTEEN

VINLAND

As Leif's ship sailed up Current Fjord, Mikkel stood at the rail. Around him the men were talking. "I name this land Vinland for its natural qualities," Leif had said after seeing the grapes.

Vinland.

Mikkel liked the sound of it. But where did Vinland begin, and where did it end? Mikkel wasn't sure. He liked to think of it as an entire area, not just one place. He only knew that abundance, great abundance, seemed to surround them wherever they went.

Leif's ship was full of logs—valuable hardwoods the men had taken from Hóp. At one time Mikkel would have thought only about the wages he would receive when they returned to Greenland. Now, instead, he wanted to stay in this new world. Each day that passed took them closer to the time when he must take Bree home to Ireland.

Until she explained, Tully had been only a name to Mikkel. I look like him? Bree thought she was saving Tully from drowning, and it was me? And because she saved me from drowning, I was able to lead the raid?

Even now, after their weeks in Hóp, the memory of Bree's pain still upset Mikkel. For as long as he could remember, his father, Sigurd, had taught him to see the cause and effect of whatever he did.

"If you do this, that will happen," Sigurd often said. "If you make a different choice, something else will happen." Because of the hurt he saw in Bree's eyes, Mikkel knew the truth of those words.

Often he had heard Bree and Devin talk about the courage to win. How could he possibly have the courage to take Bree home? Without doubt she would wed Tully. With every breath, Mikkel's heart and mind cried out, "No! No! No!"

Then, as he stood at the rail, Devin came to stand next to him. "Thank you, Mikkel," he said quietly. "In all the time we were in Hóp, you watched out for Bree. But you watched from a distance. I respect you for it."

It was true. In all those days Mikkel hadn't spoken to Bree except to wish her happy birthday. And for good reason.

"I did what you said," he told Devin. "I asked Bree about Tully. And I didn't like her answer."

"She never told you how she feels?"

"Not this way. She told me through her eyes. She used to hate me. Now she just avoids me."

Devin nodded. "You took away her home, her family, four years of her life. And you've taken her away—"

"From Tully!" Mikkel spit out the name. Though he had never met the young man who was Devin's friend, Mikkel had started to hate him.

Devin grinned. "So, you really do understand."

"I understand." Mikkel's voice was grim. "And I told Bree again that I would take both of you to Ireland. That when we leave here, I will take you straight home."

A startled look crossed Devin's face. "She didn't tell me."

Mikkel thought he knew why. "She doesn't believe me."

Courage, Mikkel thought again. This was going to require more courage than he ever had in his life. How could he do something really difficult because it was the right thing to do? How could he face the biggest test of his life by drawing on a strength that he didn't have?

And how could he possibly act with courage when everything in his heart said no?

When Leif's ship reached his camp, they found that Thorstein and his crew had completed the work that needed to be done on the houses before winter. Before long they would take both ships out of the water and check them for loose or rusted rivets.

The moment he could leave, Mikkel headed for the high sandstone ridge south of the houses. Across the grassy area with scattered trees he ran, going faster and faster. The pounding of his feet reminded him of the pounding Bree had taken—the hardships she faced because of his raid. By the time he reached the fir, birch, and alder at the bottom of the ridge he decided he had to do something about it.

Early on, Mikkel had found the quickest way across the top of the ridge. From there he climbed down on the side next to the fjord of currents. Some of the rocks dropped straight into the water. Others lay scattered here and there, rising above the waves. But Mikkel went straight to the place he liked best—the slanted rock where he could sit and look across the water to the distant coastline and the open sea.

Today the waves crashed against the shore, spraying up as though trying to reach the highest possible rock. As Mikkel thought about his promise to Bree, the thrashing waves matched his feelings.

How could he go on with his life if he took her back to Ireland? But if he really cared about Bree, shouldn't he want the best for her? Not second best, or third, or fourth, but the very best?

From the depths of his heart Mikkel felt unwilling to

give up what he wanted most. Yet if he didn't do what was best for Bree how could he ever respect himself?

In that moment Mikkel knew he had no choice. "All right, God," he said. "I can't change what I've already done. But I want the rest of my life to have some kind of purpose."

Again Mikkel held back. Again he knew he must say it all. "Some reason for living, even if I have to live without Bree."

Standing up, Mikkel faced into the wind off the sea. When peace finally stole into his heart, he started back to Leif's Camp.

That night Mikkel decided something else. Though he couldn't give back the years he took from Bree when she became a slave, he wanted to help her in whatever way he could. And he knew where to begin.

Whenever Bree managed to slip away to talk with Devin she crossed the stream by leaping from one stone to another. It wouldn't take much for her to fall, especially if it turned cold and the stones became icy.

The next evening after the men finished work for the day, Mikkel started building a bridge. When he asked Garth and some other men for help with laying two long poles across the stream, Mikkel never explained. Garth never asked why. He seemed to know.

Then Mikkel cut short, smaller logs from young trees. Using spruce root cords, he bound the short logs onto the supporting poles.

When he was done, Mikkel felt proud of his bridge. Even more, he liked how Bree felt about it.

"Thank you, Mikkel," she said quietly. It was the first time she had spoken to him since her birthday. "When winter comes——"

Yes, when winter comes.

But winter, as they knew it in Greenland, never came. Instead, the days in which it was possible to work outdoors continued.

Already Thorstein's men had cut long lengths of tree trunks to build two ramps. After stripping off the bark, they laid the lengths parallel to each other and from the edge of the water to where they wanted the ship for winter. Men had also cut shorter lengths—about four or five feet long—and stripped them of bark. These served as rollers.

When all was ready, a great number of men climbed into the stern of Leif's ship. Their weight lifted the prow to start it on the rollers. With his great strength Leif led the other men in pushing the hull up the incline. Soon the entire keel came out of the water. Working together, the men pulled Thorstein's ship onto land the same way.

In the days that followed, men checked every inch of the hulls. Each time they found rusted or broken rivets they replaced them, making sure that there would be no weak places for seawater to enter. When Leif and Thorstein were finally satisfied that the hulls were watertight, the men covered each ship with a heavy cloth tied down with walrus-hide rope.

While Devin worked in the smithy, Mikkel repaired one of the small boats in the lean-to off Leif's house. In November, then December and January, everyone expected cold winds and snow to howl down from the north. But the temperature never dropped below freezing. To those who had lived in Greenland it seemed unbelievable to have such warm weather.

During the evenings when the men sat around the long hearth in Leif's house, they played games and told stories of the valiant deeds of men from the North.

I've changed! Mikkel thought as he listened to them. Not long ago he had wanted to be one of the great Vikings. A merchant, a shrewd bargainer, the master of a ship that crossed the oceans of the world. Now that he was well on his way to that kind of wealth he wanted something different. A home. A family. Peace in his life. But instead of peace, uneasy thoughts kept edging into his mind.

When Devin told stories, Mikkel tried to learn what it was like to live in Ireland. More often Devin played his panpipes. Sometimes his tunes sounded like the march of a triumphant army. Other times Mikkel heard the rustling of tall grasses blowing in the wind at Hóp. But he always knew when Devin was thinking of home. Then he played the high clear notes and gentle tunes that reminded Mikkel of the mists of Ireland. Mists that settled on the green slopes of the Wicklow Mountains.

Each time those mountains came to mind, Mikkel pushed the thought away. How could he remember those mists? When he saw those slopes he had been thinking about how to lead the raid. How to gain the greatest possible amount of wealth.

Now those memories made Mikkel afraid. How quickly the peaceful Irish countryside could change with his return. What would happen when he set foot on the green sod of Ireland? Could he possibly get Bree home safely? See her restored to her family? And would he be able to escape to his home in Norway?

Deep inside, Mikkel felt only dread. He knew too well all that could happen.

Filled with restlessness, he followed Devin when he left Leif's house. Outside they found Bree sitting on the terrace, looking up at the sky. When Mikkel started to leave, Devin said, "No, wait. Stay with us."

Mikkel glanced at him, surprised. Something was bothering Devin, and Mikkel couldn't guess what it was.

Across the bay and open sea, rays of light filled the northern sky. High overhead, white lights merged with green. Red and purple lights blended with the other colors. As Devin and Mikkel sat down next to Bree, long shafts of light streaked upward.

As the northern lights flickered and danced, Bree caught her breath. "Our light is so small," she said softly. "A stone hollowed out in the center to hold oil. Small wicks to lighten dark rooms. And this is so big."

"But your light is very large."

Surprised, Bree turned to Mikkel.

"Our longhouses at home are dark and smoky," he said. "These sod houses—we must be warm, but there is little light."

Bree agreed. "It's why I go outside whenever I can."

But Mikkel went on. "Wherever you are, you bring light. If it hadn't been for you and Dev, I don't know what would have happened to me."

Bree giggled. "You'd still be the arrogant master of a ship. Remember what you said? 'Never forget that I am Mikkel, son of the mighty chieftain of Aurland Fjord.'"

Even Mikkel laughed.

During a rare moment when there was no one else in Leif's house, Mikkel knelt down in front of his sea chest. At the very bottom was a package wrapped round and round with sealskin. Taking it out, Mikkel pulled off the layers until he held up a book with a white calfskin cover. The light of the long fire at the center of the room caught the sparkle of precious gems.

As many times as Mikkel had seen the cover, he never stopped feeling amazed by its beauty. Running his hand over the calfskin, he lightly touched each jewel. Then he carefully opened the pages.

The bright colors and beautiful designs seemed to leap from the hand-drawn letters and pictures. Even in the dark room, light shone from the pages. As often before, Mikkel wished that he could read the words and know what they meant.

Then suddenly the door opened and Devin came in. Quickly Mikkel drew the wrapping over the book.

"No, please. Can I see it?" Devin asked. "Bree told me about it. She said it's the book of the four Gospels from the monastery."

The book stolen from the monastery, Mikkel thought when Devin did not say it. *Given to me by a monk—Bree and Devin's teacher—in exchange for the lives of his people.*

Without speaking, Mikkel held it out. With a quick swipe on his cloak, Devin wiped his hands and took the book. When he sat down on a bench, he carefully turned one page after another.

As Mikkel watched, he saw the longing in Devin's eyes. "You want to read it, don't you?"

When Devin nodded, Mikkel went on. "I know runic writing, but I can't read this."

Devin grinned. "Most people can't. It's Latin. Bree and I learned it at the Glendalough Monastery."

"Isn't it kind of strange for a girl to study at a monastery?"

Devin laughed. "That's Bree. At first I taught her.

Then she decided she wanted to go herself. It's not impossible for—" Devin stopped.

"It's not impossible for an Irish girl to go to school?" Mikkel asked. "Others have done it?"

"All over Ireland we have monasteries with good schools," Devin told him. "Students can go for a small payment, or for nothing, if they're poor. But we have other schools too. In good weather their classes are often held outside."

"But Bree? Could *any* girl go to a monastery?"

Devin closed the book with the white cover. "When we don't need to work, I'll tell you what this says."

He's guarding his tongue, Mikkel thought. *I wonder what it is that Dev doesn't want me to know?*

Though the winter months passed, it was a season in which there was no frost. To everyone's surprise the grass barely withered. Then on a morning in early March, Mikkel felt a new warmth in the air.

Eager to be out-of-doors, he left Leif's house early to run in the cool air off the sea. On this day he followed what had become a well-worn path to the end of the beak-shaped point. As he ran, the sun rose, creating a pathway of light over the sea.

Soon Leif would ask them to lower his ship into the water. There the long overlapping boards would swell and become watertight again. Leif's crew would load the timber they had cut and take their valuable cargo to Greenland. But Mikkel did not want to think of leaving here.

Nor did he want to think beyond this time. Once they reached Greenland he could no longer put off taking Bree and Devin to Ireland.

During the night a great stretch of ice had drifted down from the north. The large floe lay close to the shore of the bay, and that's where Mikkel spotted the polar bear. Instantly he stopped, waited, and watched from a distance.

While in Greenland, Mikkel had heard about polar bears, and he wasn't taking any chances. Though big and clumsy looking, they could move quickly and run very fast. Often they waited, their thick golden-white coats blending with the snow and ice, until they pounced on their prey. That prey could include humans.

Now and then the bear turned his long, narrow head, and Mikkel saw his small ears and black nose. When the bear stopped his pacing and dropped down on the ice, he seemed to disappear. Often such bears hunted seals by waiting next to a breathing hole in the ice.

Bree! Instantly Mikkel knew he must warn her. If she saw adult seals on the ice, she would do her best to find a pup. That could be deadly.

But when he returned to the houses, Garth called him. Caught up in the work of the day, Mikkel didn't have a chance to talk with Bree.

FOURTEEN

SEALS UPON THE ICE

When Bree woke in the small hut she shared with Hekja, the wood cover above the smoke hole rattled in the March wind. It made Bree impatient to be outside, to feel the spring-like air that had surrounded her the day before. If she went now she could have a few precious minutes before starting the daily porridge.

Pushing aside her reindeer-hide blanket, Bree got up from the dirt floor she and Nola had covered with dried grasses. Bree dressed quietly and quickly and crept out into the gray light before dawn.

The balmy air reminded Bree of Ireland and her family. What was happening to Daddy and Mam? To her brother Adam and sisters Keely, Cara, and Jen? What would it be like when she could talk with them again?

Soon Shadow found her and followed close behind. Long ago he had learned that if he went along on her early-morning walks, he had to be quiet. He also had to obey.

In the rare times when Bree was free to slip away she sometimes followed the stream to the lake behind the houses. More often she went to the rocky ridge. The moment she stepped down on the far side no one could see her from the houses. No one could give her more work.

By now Bree had gone there often enough to know the quickest way through the bushes, fir, and birch at the foot of the ridge. Carefully picking her way, she climbed the steep slope and crossed the grass and rocks along the top. When Bree stood on the ridge, looking east, she saw the first glimmer of light along the horizon.

As though she were home, her love of that moment welled up inside Bree. Countless times she had climbed Brockagh Mountain and waited for the sun to rise above the Irish Sea. But now, afraid that someone would notice her on the ridge, Bree dropped down on the other side.

When Bree reached her favorite rock, she gazed across the fjord of currents. Below where she stood, a great mass of drift ice had lodged against the high rocky shore. In the half-light before dawn some of the ice looked flat. In other places it had piled up, as though pushed by the wind into ridges and chunks. In still other places smaller ice floes had separated from the large mass and drifted in the current.

To Bree's delight she saw seals. Even in the half-light their coats were dark against the ice and easy to pick out. Where there were adult seals, there had to be pups, and Bree wanted to find one. How could it be easier?

As she climbed down the boulders to the edge of the fjord, Shadow followed her. When she told him to stay, he whimpered and wagged his tail. But when she told him a second time, he obeyed. Stepping onto the ice, Bree started toward an adult seal.

It was near open water, but the ice seemed safe enough. As Bree drew close to the seal, she realized that a pup lay nearby. With a fluffy white coat it was almost hidden in the ice and snow. Then Bree saw its black nose and whiskers. In the growing light the pup's round, dark eyes looked up at her.

Ahhhh! Filled with the wonder of it, Bree wanted to reach out, touch the pup. Feel its soft fur. Stroke its back as she would a favorite dog.

Just then Bree remembered Shadow. When she looked around, he sat on the rock where she had commanded him to wait. Good dog!

Bree turned back to the seals. In that moment the mother slid into the water, leaving her pup. Instantly it cried out, almost sounding like a human baby.

Not wanting to upset the pup, Bree waited. When it

grew quiet she crept closer. But then, as she stepped down on a soft piece of ice, it separated from the larger floe.

Heart in her throat, Bree tried to catch her balance. Instead, the chunk flipped up, and she plunged into the fjord.

As the water closed around her head, Bree slipped deep beneath the surface. Stretching down, she tried to touch bottom, but her foot felt nothing.

I'm a good swimmer, she told herself, trying not to panic. Kicking hard, she rose to the surface. But cold seized her body, sent prickles through her limbs.

Pain in her chest, Bree gasped, choked on a mouthful of water. With great gulps she fought for air.

"Help!" she cried, and Shadow started to bark. Running along the rocks, he barked at the sea.

Turning back to the ice, Bree tried to swim toward it. Could she reach the edge, grab hold, climb out?

Already the current had swept her from the nearest floe. Her cloak pulled her down. With numb fingers Bree tugged at the ring-pin, let the cloth fall away.

"Help!" she cried again. "Shadow, get Dev!" But the dog raced back and forth on the rocks, barking without stopping. As if from a faraway place, Bree heard him and didn't understand what it meant.

As she struggled to think, Bree remembered. No one knew where she was. No one would hear her cries for help.

Each time Bree tried to lift her arms, they felt too heavy to move. Her long wool dress caught her legs, weighed her down. When the water closed around her again, the light disappeared. Then her ears pounded.

Frantic now, she spun in the darkness, kicked, and kicked again. Fighting her way up, she surfaced and gasped for air.

Shore. Rocks. Where was shore? Somewhere she had seen it. Then in some dim part of her mind, she knew. It didn't matter that she was a strong swimmer. In the icy water it wouldn't be enough.

Once more Bree cried out. "Help! Help!" But who could possibly hear? Her words were only a faint croak.

Then the current caught her, sending her farther downstream. This time she cried out to God.

In the darkness of Leif's house, Mikkel lay on his sleeping bench and could not sleep. He had wakened to one thought. *Now is the time.*

Soon after his raid in Ireland, he had learned that the wrong person could open the padlock on his sea chest. At the first opportunity Mikkel built a new hiding place for the treasure that made him wealthy at the age of fourteen. Now he hid his riches in full view of the world. How many people had looked at a simple keg without knowing the treasure it contained?

But four years had passed. In that time the wood had dried, and the long, narrow slat—the stave that hid his secret place—slid open too easily. What if someone picked up the keg the wrong way? What if the two bags of silver coins and the bag of gems he borrowed from the Glendalough Monastery spilled out?

Borrowed. Mikkel had used the word for so long that it came without thought. *Stole, Mikkel. Be honest with yourself.*

Long ago his father, Sigurd, had sent him off with a trusted friend. Hauk was to teach Mikkel to be the master of a ship and a skillful merchant. But while Hauk was sick, Mikkel led his crew in the raid on the monastery. Then he returned home to an angry father.

"Unless you find a way to set your actions right, you'll be a slave to what you have done," Sigurd had told him.

"Me? I'm not a slave," Mikkel replied. "I'm a free man, just like you."

"No!" Sigurd answered. "You're a slave to whatever you serve."

In the time since, Mikkel had been forced to face the truth of his father's words. Not only had Bree and the other Irish been hurt by his desire for wealth; because Hammer was not willing to forget that raid, it had nearly cost Mikkel his life.

The time is now, he thought again. *Now.* Whether he

liked it or not. If he was going to be free, he had to set things right. But he also had to fix his keg when no one could see what he was doing.

Sitting up, Mikkel swung his feet to the dirt floor and dressed quickly. In his belt he put his knife and a small ax. Throwing his cloak over his shoulders, he fastened it with a ring-pin. Then he picked up his keg, staves from another keg made at the same time, and some coils of spruce root. While everyone else slept, he slipped out the door.

A short distance from Leif's house, Mikkel stopped to tie the spruce roots around the keg. Leaving the ends long, he slung the keg onto his back and tied the cords across his chest and around his waist. With the extra staves under one arm, he started running.

When he reached the bottom of the steep slope he noticed the outline of a path between the trees and bushes. Who else came this way besides himself?

In the gray light before dawn he kept running, never slowing when the slope grew steep. By now Mikkel knew a safe path between the rocks on the top of the ridge.

He was partway across the ridge when he felt a breeze off the sea. Then he heard a cry.

At first he thought he was mistaken. It had to be seals or some other animal. Without slowing down, Mikkel listened. Above the sounds of the sea the cry seemed human. This time he heard a dog bark. Shadow!

Shadow? It could only be Bree needing help. Without letting up, the dog kept barking.

Leaping forward, Mikkel ran still faster, heading for the sound. Then in the growing light he saw it. The ice floe lodged against the rocks. The seals on the ice.

Again Mikkel heard Shadow's bark. Then he saw the dog, racing back and forth along the rocks, barking at the water. Bree in open, ice-filled water. Bree crying, "Help! Help!"

"Bree!" he called, as he started down over the rocks. "Bree!"

For one moment she turned her head, looked up.

"Swim for shore!" For one instant Mikkel was sure she heard. As though her arms were weighted, Bree tried to raise them. But when her hands fell back, Mikkel knew what was wrong.

The cold. The ice. In minutes Bree would be gone. Though a strong swimmer, she could not win over the cold.

In one swift movement Mikkel dropped the staves he carried and tore the keg off his back. In the next moment he threw off his cloak. *The keg. It's her only hope.*

Clutching it in his hands, he ran as fast as he could. "Bree! Bree!"

Dropping down over the rocks, Mikkel raced to the edge of the fjord. When he reached the rocks next to the water, Mikkel stopped.

His fingers clumsy with his need to hurry, he took the cord from one end of the keg and tied it to the other cord. Even together, the cords weren't long enough. And Bree was almost gone, too cold to fight much longer.

Then Mikkel saw it. The current. In that short space of time the current had taken Bree closer to shore. And there just a bit farther on, rocks reaching further into the fjord. Could he get there in time?

Running again, he called all the while. "Bree! Kick for the rocks! Bree! I'm coming!"

Once he stumbled and almost fell. Once he nearly lost his foot in a crevice.

Then he reached it—the flattest rock he could find. "Bree!"

As she turned her head toward the sound of his voice he called again. "I'll throw a keg in front of you. Catch it!"

One nod. One movement of her head as if she understood. But the terror of it all filled Mikkel.

If he threw the keg even a short distance from her, she wouldn't be able to get there. If he threw too close, the keg could hit her head with deadly results.

Quickly Mikkel tied the end of the cord around his wrist. Standing still, he took careful aim. "Bree!" he called again, and threw the keg.

FIFTEEN

COURAGE TO WIN?

The keg splashed into the water two arm lengths in front of Bree. Could she get there?

Then Bree's hands reached out. Her arms wrapped around the wood.

"Hang on!" Mikkel shouted. "I'll pull you in! Just hang on! Kick!"

Hand over hand, he pulled the cord. Steady. Strong. No sudden jerks.

Once Bree almost lost the keg. "Hang on!" he called. "You're making it! Keep coming!"

Now he could see the paleness of her face. Mikkel pulled and pulled again. At last she was close enough to reach.

Grabbing her upper arm, Mikkel pulled her onto the rock, took the keg from her, set it down. With a slash of his knife he cut the cord from his wrist.

Bree's face looked blue now and her body trembled. Gathering her into his arms, Mikkel threw her over his shoulder and headed up the rocks.

He had gone only a few steps when she spoke through chattering teeth. "What about your keg?"

"Forget it!" he said. "You're more important."

When he reached his cloak, he wrapped it around Bree, threw her over his shoulder again, and started running.

With her every shiver Mikkel felt the cold. By now Bree was trembling so hard that her entire body shook.

"Where am I?" she murmured once. And then, "The baby seal. Soft. White. I want to hold the baby seal."

With every ounce of his strength, Mikkel ran even faster.

"The water. It's so cold." She sounded drowsy now.

Mikkel was halfway to the houses before he noticed that Shadow ran alongside him, still barking.

"Mikkel?" Bree's voice seemed to come from a far country. "Is that you?"

"It's me."

"But we're in Ireland. How can you be in Ireland?"

When people heard Shadow they came running. "Get Dev," Mikkel told one of them.

Without stopping, Mikkel hurried to the house where Bree lived. Nola held open the door. Stepping inside,

Mikkel looked around. "Where's her sleeping bench?"

"Put her there," Nola told Mikkel, pointing to the bench closest to the fire. "What happened?"

"She fell into the fjord," Mikkel said. When he laid Bree down, her eyes fluttered open, but her entire body continued to shake.

"I'll take care of her," Nola promised. "Send Hekja here."

Mikkel headed for the door, then turned back to build up the fire. Then he made sure the cooking pot was full of hot water.

Partway to the door, Mikkel stopped again. At different times he had seen two men fall into a sea filled with ice. Though both were rescued, one man had died and the other lived. Everyone talked about it because the man who died was much stronger, more healthy, than the one who lived.

It frightened Mikkel. What if, even after being rescued, Bree died? Why had one man lived and the other hadn't?

Mikkel struggled to remember. Then he knew he really didn't know. He only remembered what people said.

"I need to get her out of those cold clothes," Nola told him, as if trying to hurry him to the door. "It's good I have plenty of hot water."

That's it! Mikkel thought. Though he couldn't be really sure if he knew what was best, he had to try.

"The water shouldn't be hot," he said. "Warm her slowly. Gradually."

As Mikkel stopped next to the bench where Bree lay, her eyes fluttered open.

"Mikkel? It's you?" she asked again through chattering teeth.

"It's me."

Though she was still shaking all over, a faint smile touched Bree's lips. Then her eyes closed.

As soon as he sent Hekja to Nola, Mikkel dropped down on the grass outside Garth's house. Bowing his head, he shut out everything and everyone else around him. He wanted only to pray.

When he found Mikkel, Devin could barely speak. "Bree fell into the sea?"

"Current Fjord." Mikkel didn't understand all that had happened. He knew only that there had been seals on the ice. Knowing Bree, she probably wanted to see the seals. "She must have fallen off the ice."

"That's how you found her? Already in the water? The fjord of strong currents?"

Elbows on his knees, head supported by his hands, Mikkel nodded again.

"Nola won't let me in," Devin said.

When Mikkel lifted his head, he looked into his friend's eyes. "Dev, it was the most awful thing I've ever seen in my whole life."

For the rest of the day and into the evening Mikkel waited outside the house. Each time he drew a breath he wondered if Bree was drawing hers. What would happen to her?

It was Nola who let in Devin first, and later Mikkel, to see her. Without making a sound, Mikkel sat down near the sleeping bench where Bree lay.

An oil lamp with three wicks flickered in the dark room. Bree lay with her eyes closed, quiet and still.

For a long time Mikkel sat there, glad only to watch the sealskin blanket move up and down with her breathing. Glad only to listen and know that no raspy cough held her tight in its grip. And then, at last, her eyes opened.

"Thank you, Mikkel." Her voice was hoarse, but the most welcome sound he had ever heard.

"Don't mention it."

"I will. I could have—"

"I know. I'm glad I heard you call. That I was close enough to help."

"I was never so frightened in my whole life. In only a few more minutes—"

"Don't think about it."

"I can't help but think about it," she said. "It could have all been over so quickly. In the moment I thought I was gone, I had just one question. Have I done everything I'm supposed to do in life?"

Mikkel laughed. "I hope not. You're only seventeen."

"I'm serious, Mikkel. I was so close to death, and the thought came in an instant. I want to be the person God wants me to be."

"Me too," Mikkel said quietly. Then he realized how strongly he meant it. "Me too."

Reaching out, he put one hand over hers. "Let's not ever forget that."

For a while she was silent, as though unable to speak. As she lay with closed eyes one tear wet her cheek. Then she looked up.

"You were afraid too," Bree said softly. "But you knew what to do. And you did it. That's courage, Mikkel. The courage to win."

Now it was Mikkel who was unable to speak.

When Mikkel's cloak was dry, Nola returned it to him. Only then did Mikkel remember how he had thrown aside the ring-pin when he pulled off his cloak. And it was more than a day later before Mikkel thought about his keg.

Like a bolt of lightning he remembered he had left it on a boulder on the edge of Straumfjord, the fjord of strong currents. It would take only one thrashing wave, one powerful splash, and his wealth would be gone forever.

"What about your keg?" Bree had asked when he pulled her from the water.

"Forget it," he had said. "You're more important."

Now, remembering, Mikkel knew a freedom he hadn't felt since his raid on the monastery. As he set out for the rocky ridge, he walked slowly instead of running.

"You're more important, Bree," he whispered, wanting to say it again. Whatever happened in the time ahead, that would still be true, even if she married Tully.

When he found the keg sitting just where he left it, Mikkel couldn't believe it. As he picked it up, he touched the gash in the wood—the gash he made four long years ago.

He and Bree had argued, as they usually did. Her questions about the dragon at the front of his ship made him angry.

"If you think that stupid dragon at the front of your ship will protect you, you're wrong," she said as Mikkel worked in his boathouse.

Suddenly his ax slipped, making the gash in the wood. The stave for the keg was already finished. Because he didn't have time to make another, he used the damaged piece.

Now as Mikkel touched the gash, the stave slid open easily, revealing the hiding place he had built. It was a miracle, he knew, that the loose piece hadn't opened in the water, spilling out his treasure.

But for Mikkel there was an even bigger miracle. Before leaving Greenland, Bree had found his secret hid-

ing place. Even though she was close to drowning, cling-
ing to the keg, she must have felt the gash in its side. Why
else would she ask, "What about your keg?"

And he had said, "You're more important, Bree."
Whatever happened between them in the time ahead,
Mikkel knew he would always feel grateful for his answer.

After a quick search he found the four-year-old staves
he had thrown on the ground. Sitting down, he began to
work.

When he finished, there was a new stave covering the
secret place. With a tighter fit, it could only be opened a
certain way. But as he looked at the keg, he stopped,
thought for a moment, and sat down again.

Carefully he made a gash in the new stave. A gash that
looked just like the old one. If needed, Bree could find
the treasure again. If something happened to him, she
would know what to do.

SIXTEEN

THE WARNING

At first Nola kept Bree inside, simply saying, "She needs to recover." When Bree started cooking again, she seemed quiet, thoughtful, and not like herself. Mikkel couldn't help but wonder if she was feeling all right.

One day he returned to the rocky ridge, looked out over the fjord of strong currents, and felt grateful that Bree was alive. But still, it would be a relief if she would just get angry and throw out her words in every direction.

While there, he looked around for his ring-pin. Wherever he had tossed it, the pin had probably fallen between rocks, never to be seen again. Or maybe someone had picked it up. Mikkel missed the bronze pin because it held his cloak in place but also because he had gotten it in Dublin.

"I'll make you a new one," Devin offered, and he did. When he wasn't making nails, he pounded out a ring-pin.

When he gave it to Mikkel, Devin acted as if it was of no importance. But Mikkel ran his hand over the smooth surface and said, "It's nice. Thanks, Dev. When I use it, I'll remember you."

For a moment their eyes met. Then Mikkel looked away. Before long they would part, and Mikkel wished it didn't have to be so.

When the danger of damage from ice floes was past, Leif and Thorstein were eager to get their ships into the water. Removing the walrus-hide ropes, their crews took off the heavy cloths they had used to cover the ships. When all was ready, a number of men climbed into Leif's ship.

They had pulled it out of the water prow first. Now as they stood in the bow the stern lifted off the logs on which the ship had been stored. Leif and some of the other men on the ground pushed at the sides of the ship. Soon it started to slide down the ramp of logs. With a splash it settled in the water.

After setting the mast in place and rigging the sail, the men also lowered Thorstein's ship into the water.

As Mikkel started back to the houses, his gaze fell upon long grasses glistening with dew in the morning sun. Then Mikkel saw something. Nearby, tucked between large rocks, beautiful blue flowers were opening.

Bree! was Mikkel's first thought. *I must show them to Bree!* But then he remembered his promise to keep his distance from her. *No, I can't.*

"I don't want you marrying my sister," Dev had said. "If Bree ever gets home, she needs to come back to our family—our life there. She needs to marry an Irish lad."

Except for when he needed to save Bree's life, Mikkel had kept his promise to his friend. Again, Mikkel found it very hard. Watch Bree from a distance? With all his heart he wanted to bring her here. To show her these reminders of spring. But if he did, he would break his promise to Devin.

When Mikkel knew the answer he didn't like it. But as he kept on toward Leif's house, he met Devin.

"I found some blue flowers Bree would like," Mikkel said quickly before he could change his mind. Turning, he pointed back to the place near the bay. "Maybe they'll help her be strong again."

"I'll bring some to her," Devin said.

When he clapped Mikkel on the shoulder, Devin looked into his eyes. In that moment Mikkel knew that Devin understood how much he wanted to give Bree the flowers himself. And how hard it was for Mikkel to keep his promise.

When Devin brought the flowers to her, Bree reached out, gently touching the nearest petal. She knew where they had grown—in a cranny between rocks, close to the bay.

"They're beautiful," she said, her voice filled with awe.

In her mind's eye she could see the grasses nearby and the blue petals trembling in the wind. "They're a small iris," she said as she took the short stems. "Thanks, Dev. Thanks for bringing them to me."

Then Bree could hold her thoughts no longer. They started as a giggle deep inside. When she tried not to laugh, Devin stared at her.

"What's wrong?" he asked.

But the laughter filled Bree's heart, bubbled up, and spilled over. As Devin watched, he too, laughed, and soon, like the children they once were, they laughed at each other.

Finally Devin said, "Now what was that all about?"

Bree giggled again and looked him straight in the eye. "Dev, you have been my brother for seventeen and a half years. You are now nineteen and you have never given me flowers before. Mikkel told you to do this, didn't he?"

Unable to stop herself, Bree giggled again. "When we get back to Ireland, remember. Flowers will be important to your true love. Lil really likes flowers. But you don't have to give them to your sister."

When a flush of embarrassment washed across Devin's face, Bree said no more. But of one thing she felt sure. Her brother would wait for Lil to grow up.

As soon as Devin left, Bree put the flowers in water. Again she saw the cranny where they belonged and the petals trembling in the wind. "Thanks, Mikkel," she whispered.

From then on Bree was her old self again.

For some time Bree had seen Mikkel and Devin walk away from the houses, talking together when they finished their work. But she had forgotten about them on the evening when she walked to the long flat point reaching out into the sea.

By now, Bree was well acquainted with this land she called Beak Point. From here she could see in every direction. To the north and east lay the endless stretch of the ocean. In the early morning she watched the sun rise over the water. During the evening, the sun set at different places, depending on the season. On December 21, its orange-red light had shone through a gap in the rocks on the high ridge.

On that spring evening Bree found Devin and Mikkel sitting close to the end of the point. When Bree started to back away, Devin called her. "Come on. Sit down."

In that moment Bree noticed that Devin held a large

book with precious gems on the calfskin cover. "You have Brother Cronan's book with you?" she asked Mikkel. Bree thought he had left it in Norway.

As though there had been no interruption, Devin started talking again. After reading a line or two from the book, he translated it into Norse for Mikkel. Then Devin explained what the words meant.

Always the older brother who looked out for his sister, Devin had helped Bree the same way. Now he needed only to say something once, and Mikkel had it memorized. And Mikkel, like Bree before him, never stopped asking questions.

While the sun dropped low over the water, Devin told Mikkel about the Saul who became Paul. "He came from a noble family," Devin explained. "He was a leading young man of his time, and he made it his job to persecute Christians. When they fled before him, Saul went from town to town, seeking out believers he could take as prisoners. A man named Stephen was stoned to death, and Saul watched and approved."

As Devin spoke, Mikkel grew still, as if trying to hide his feelings. But Devin went on. "One day, as Saul traveled to another city, a light from heaven flashed around him. Blinded by the light, Saul fell to the ground and heard Jesus speak. 'Saul, Saul, why do you persecute Me?'

'Who are You, Lord?' Saul asked.

"When he got up, the men traveling with him led

Saul by the hand into the city. Three days later, God sent a man to pray with Saul and restored his sight. He became the teacher we call Paul—a man who took long, dangerous journeys to tell people what he believed. He sailed on the Mediterranean Sea."

"I know it!" Mikkel broke in. "I know Norwegians who have sailed that sea!"

"This same Paul died because of his faith."

"He suffered," Mikkel said, as if he knew the end of the story. "He suffered in order to do what he believed."

Suddenly Mikkel leaped up. Without a backward look he walked away, his long legs reaching out as if he wanted only to be far distant from them.

"That was too much for him," Bree said quietly.

"Maybe," answered Devin, his eyes thoughtful. "Maybe not."

"Have you told him the story before?"

Devin shook his head. "Maybe Leif did. But I think Mikkel senses something he isn't telling us."

As they watched, Mikkel walked to the other side of the bay. Between them, the waters of the sea rushed toward shore, bringing whitecaps on each wave. As the waves crashed against the rocks, Mikkel stood for a long time just looking at the pounding surf.

"Dev," Bree said. "Remember how you helped me before I was captured as a slave?"

They had been rowing downriver, returning home,

when he reminded her of something they started when they were young children. When Devin faced a bully, Bree folded her arms across her chest as a signal. Without words she told him, "Courage to win, Dev. I'm praying for you."

"I remember," Devin said, and Bree went on. "You've helped Mikkel the same way, as though you're preparing him for what's ahead. But what's going to happen when you're no longer with him?"

Dev shook his head, not answering.

"Will he be a strong, courageous leader?" Bree asked. "Or will he leave behind everything he's learned?"

When they started back to the houses they were agreed on one thing. Both of them cared deeply about what would happen to Mikkel.

Though he tried with all his might to push it aside, Mikkel knew. Each time he did his best to ignore the warning, it returned to him. Now as he looked across the windswept bay, he had to face it. A hard time lay ahead of him. There would be suffering. Suffering unlike anything he had ever known.

To make things even worse, he was afraid of what that suffering could involve. It was hard to imagine anything worse than seeing Bree almost drown. Yet if something happened to her when he tried to bring her home, he wouldn't be able to live with himself.

A week later, when Mikkel left Leif's house after the late-day meal, the fog had rolled in from the sea. The moist air settled around him and clung to his hair and beard. In the strange, half-white light the rocks along the shore loomed large. But Mikkel was nearly upon them before he saw their dark shape.

He had forgotten his ax on Leif's ship. In the damp air he didn't want to leave it outside overnight. Now he walked quickly up the ramp and found it. Slipping the ax into the holder on his belt, he turned, ready to leave. But something didn't seem right.

Walking to the bow, Mikkel peered into the fog. Like a wall it lay before him. A wall that hid everything around him. The fog seemed to put him in a space apart, yet also closed him in. Even the gentle lapping of waves against the shore sounded loud.

Eerie. As though not attached to anything.

Standing there, Mikkel tried to think why he felt uneasy. There seemed no explanation for it, only a fear he couldn't name. But there it was again. From deep within a sense of warning. What was it?

Yet as he listened, he heard no sound except the lapping of the waves.

I'm getting jumpy, Mikkel told himself. But when he tried to shrug it off, he couldn't.

No sound. No grating of a soft leather shoe on pebbles of the beach. Instead, a fog as thick as heavy smoke.

No sound. Someone who moved as silently as a cat.

Suddenly Mikkel knew. In the next instant he whirled around. But it was too late.

SEVENTEEN

WHEN THE WIND BLOWS FAIR

Only three feet away, Hammer stood before him. One arm's length away, he waited. But as Mikkel faced him, Hammer said, "I won't hurt you."

Alert and watchful, Mikkel stood there, ready to defend himself.

"I won't hurt you," Hammer said again.

As Mikkel looked into his eyes, he knew that Hammer spoke truth. "Let's talk," he said.

They sat down on the deck, facing each other. When Mikkel studied the man before him, he saw something else. Hammer's anger and resentment were gone.

Then he spoke. "You gave me hope. You helped me believe I can have a future."

"I did? When?"

"At Hóp. I hated you. You remind me of my brother Garth—successful in everything you do."

Mikkel laughed. "You've got that wrong. It might be true of Garth, but not of me." If there was anything Mikkel had learned since the raid, it was that.

"He's a good farmer," Hammer said. "Leif's best carpenter. A storyteller everyone wants to hear—"

But Mikkel broke in. "Maybe he's a good storyteller because you always listened."

Hammer blinked. But then his shoulders shifted, and Mikkel knew. Though the fog hid it now, Hammer would walk taller.

In that moment Mikkel remembered the day they worked together in the woods. Wanting to talk about what happened during the raid, he told Hammer, "I know why you hate me."

"No, you don't," Hammer said.

"I do," Mikkel answered. "I know why you want revenge." But Hammer didn't care to hear. In all this time they had never talked about it.

Now Mikkel said, "There's something you need to know. When I planned the raid on the monastery, I had a reason for saying you must guard the ship. I didn't want you to kill someone."

"That's why you kept me there? I thought you wanted everything for yourself."

"I did." Mikkel had to be honest with himself. "I divided some of it, but not everything. I wanted to be a wealthy man, but I didn't want anyone hurt. I was afraid you'd forget how strong you are."

As though unable to take it in, Hammer stared at him. "You wanted silver coins."

"Yes."

"You wanted gems."

Mikkel nodded.

"But you didn't want to kill anyone? And you thought I would?"

"If you got angry. If someone stood in your way. If you forgot how strong you are."

"Maybe I would have." As though unable to face the thought, Hammer covered his face with his hands. When he finally spoke, his voice was muffled. "You're right. I would have killed people. And I would have been sorry the rest of my life. You saved me from that."

For a long time Hammer sat there, his face hidden. Finally he looked up. "Mikkel?"

Hammer paused, then seemed to force himself to go on. "When I tried to hurt you—"

Tried to kill me, Mikkel thought.

"I had finally learned where you hide your horde." Mikkel nodded. "I figured that out."

"But I won't try to take it again. You don't have to keep covering your back."

Mikkel grinned. So Hammer knew, after all.

"You've changed, Mikkel. If you can change that much, I can change too."

Each day Leif's men did more of the work needed to bring home the valuable goods they had gathered. On the day they loaded the logs they had prepared at Hóp, Bree knew they would soon leave. Thorstein wanted to see more of this new world and would start back to Greenland later.

By now Bree had grown used to packing whatever was needed for a voyage—the kegs of dried fish, the cooking pots, and the water. During the winter she, Nola, and Hekja had baked flatbread and stored it in sea chests to keep it dry and crisp. Soon they'd be ready to leave.

Then came the warm summer day when Leif told them, "If the wind blows fair, we'll sail in the morning."

In the small hut she shared with Hekja, Bree packed her few belongings. In the woven basket from Nikmaq she put butternuts and shells she had picked up on the sandbars at Hóp. Then a small rock from the place where she liked to sit as she looked across Current Fjord.

The rock reminded Bree of her moments of freedom. In the piece of sandstone she saw her clear view of the fjord and the open sea. Yet there was something even more important. Whenever she remembered the terror of her near drowning, she felt sure of one miraculous gift. Mikkel had come at just the right time.

Bree set the woven basket into her sea chest, then picked up the birch bark basket. Gently, so the petals would not break apart, Bree wrapped a soft cloth around the blue iris Mikkel had wanted her to see.

By now, the petals had curled together, drying into almost nothing. The once-thick stems were a pale green. The transparent husks that supported the blooms were wheat-colored. But Bree still remembered how the flowers looked when Devin brought them to her. In her mind's eye she saw the blue petals trembling in the wind off the bay. And she remembered that they were Mikkel's gift.

With great care Bree set the flowers inside the birch bark basket. As though tucking them into a nest, she drew more soft cloths around them, then set the basket at the very top of her belongings.

As Leif's ship headed out to sea, a pathway of light shimmered on the water. Bree stood in the stern, looking back.

In their time at Leif's Camp, the bay had become a place of refuge. Where there was only a terrace, three large houses, three small buildings, and a hut for smelting iron now stood. It had been a good land, full of berries, fish, and wild game. A gateway for sailing to the tidal lagoons.

Now when Bree looked into the cargo hold she saw

the timber stripped of bark and prepared by skillful hands. In the filled boat that bobbed behind them was the proof of their grape picking—another symbol of all this new world had to offer.

When Mikkel came to stand beside her, he also looked back. "I needed to do this," he said. "I needed to know I could help with building something strong."

"You don't want to leave, do you?" Bree asked.

"It's a place of freedom." Regret filled his voice. "A place of peace. A bountiful land. A good land."

"Will you ever come back?"

"I like to think I will, but I don't know. First I will take you home."

Startled, Bree felt afraid. For over ten months, they had not spoken of the promise he made when she was so upset. Nor had they spoken of his long-ago promise to Bree and Devin. "If both of you go with me for one voyage, I'll give Bree her freedom."

In the years that had passed, Devin and Mikkel had turned nineteen. In a few more months Bree would be eighteen. Looking up, she searched Mikkel's face, then his eyes. When she spoke, her voice was hard with anger.

"Don't say that unless you really mean it," she warned. "I can't handle any more disappointment."

Mikkel's gaze held steady. "You won't need to. This is my promise to you. When we leave Greenland I will sail directly to Ireland."

"Mikkel—" Bree's voice broke. "I want to believe you. I want to trust that you will do what you say—"

"I will."

Unwilling to let him see her cry, Bree turned away. But Mikkel spoke to her back.

"I will, Bree. I promise."

For a moment he waited, then said, "You're missing something."

As Bree turned back for her last look at the houses next to the bay, the early morning sunlight rested upon their roofs.

When he spoke again, Mikkel's voice was strong. "Thank you, God, for this newfound land."

To Bree's relief they had favorable winds for the entire crossing. As they came into sight of the mountains of Greenland, she stood on the ship, looking up.

Only now when she saw the mountains from this side did Bree really understand their massive height. Dark and steep on the lower ranges next to the sea, the top of the mountains shone white with snow and ice—glaciers that extended long distances. Low-hanging clouds seemed to touch their tops, while drift ice floated in the black waters of the sea.

As Leif stood at the tiller, Mikkel spoke to him. "Why do you steer so close to the wind?"

"I'm watching my course," Leif answered. "Do you see something unusual?"

Mikkel shook his head, but Leif kept his course. Soon others started watching.

"Don't you see something unusual?" Leif asked them. Still no one did, but then Leif said, "I'm not sure whether it's a ship or a skerry I see."

"It's a skerry!" Mikkel exclaimed a few minutes later. By now, Bree could also see a small, rocky island.

With his keen eyesight Leif saw even more—there were people on the skerry. "I want to reach them," Leif said. "If they need our help, we'll give it to them. If they are hostile, we'll have all the advantages on our side."

RICH AND FAMOUS

As Leif sailed close to the rocky island, his men lowered the sail, dropped anchor, and put out the small
boat towed behind the ship.

"Who's in charge of your group?" Leif called as he
drew close.

"I am Thorir, a Norwegian merchant," said one of the
men. "And what is your name?"

"Leif Erikson."

"Are you the son of Erik the Red of Brattahlid?"

"I am, and I invite all of you to come with me. Bring
as many of your valuables as my ship can carry."

Taking a few at a time, Leif and his crew gathered the
shipwrecked people into the small boat. Trembling with

cold and exposure, the rescued people climbed gratefully on board his ship.

One of the fifteen was Thorir's wife, a young woman named Gudrid. Holding her hand, Bree led Gudrid over to the most sheltered place she could find. Quickly Bree gathered sealskins and wrapped them around Gudrid and the other survivors.

As soon as Leif's crew collected whatever they could take in his ship, they set sail again. Bree, Nola, and Hekja went from one person to the next, giving food, water, and whatever would warm them.

Struck with Gudrid's beauty, Bree soon discovered that her inner beauty was just as unusual. In spite of her ordeal, Gudrid was wise and good and knew how to act with strangers.

When his ship reached Brattahlid, the farm settled by his father, Leif invited Gudrid, Thorir, and three men from their crew into his home. Then Leif found places for the rest of the shipwrecked people so they had time to recuperate and stay over winter. No one wanted to sail when the dangerous storms came in autumn.

As Bree served the late-day meal, she heard Leif talking. Already he was looking ahead to the following summer. "Do you want to go back to Vinland?" he asked Mikkel. "You have been of much value to me."

Bree stopped, unable to move on. Mikkel liked working with Leif. He also liked the world they called Vinland.

But Bree's hands clenched, just thinking about another delay.

In that moment Mikkel glanced up and saw her listening. "I'd like to go with you," he said as he turned back to Leif. "But I've made a promise. A pledge of honor to Bree and Dev. I said I'd take them home."

To the surprise of both Bree and Devin, Mikkel made no more delays. While he had been gone, the men in his crew who stayed behind took care of his ship. Now it was ready for sailing.

As if he had often thought about what to do, Mikkel moved quickly ahead. Within three days he and his men loaded all the trade goods they had gathered, along with food and water for the journey to Ireland. Then Leif, his mother, Thjodhild, [*Turdhild*], and other Christians came together at the small church she had built.

The first Christian church in Greenland, it had become a gathering place for those who wanted to worship the true God. Today there were too many people to all fit inside. As they stood on land overlooking the fjord, Bree looked around the group.

Leif, Mikkel, Devin, Garth, Nola, even Hammer. For a moment Bree wondered what had happened to him, for Hammer seemed a different person. But it was Thjodhild that Bree watched most.

While in Greenland, she had worked alongside this woman for three years. Bree knew her strong spirit. She had been with Thjodhild when she planned and built her church. Now they were saying good-bye again.

As people prayed for the safety and good health of all those on Mikkel's ship, Bree looked up. At the same moment Devin glanced her way, tipped his head toward Mikkel, then closed his eyes again. *Dev remembers!* Bree thought.

Often they had talked about it. Mikkel was becoming a leader like his father, Sigurd. What would happen to Mikkel in the time ahead? Would he be a strong leader? Someone who walked with faith in his Lord and lived with courage when it counted most?

Then in her clear voice Thjodhild spoke. "Mikkel, the Lord Himself goes before you and will be with you. He will never leave you nor forsake you. Do not be afraid; do not be discouraged."

For a time Mikkel stood with bowed head. As he finished praying, he looked toward the fjord. His longship, the *Conquest,* lay at anchor. But Mikkel gazed beyond it, as though seeing the far reaches of the sea.

When he needed to say good-bye, Mikkel stood before Leif, looking as though he found it difficult to speak. The strong Greenlander was still taller, but they almost stood eye to eye.

"I have heard what others say of you," Mikkel told him. "That you found people on a wrecked ship and brought them home with you. That you showed yourself then, as in most other things, as a great man of a high mind who brought Christianity to Greenland. I have found all of that true."

Mikkel cleared his throat. "King Olaf asked you to do something very difficult, and you did it. Then you led us to a new world and led us safely home. I thank you, Leif. Thank you for allowing me to learn from you."

Mikkel paused and then went on. "Now I must go and do something very difficult."

For an instant Leif glanced over to Bree. Then he looked straight into Mikkel's eyes. "The Lord Himself *will* go before you. God be with you, my friend."

In the years they had lived in Greenland and the new-found land, Bree had forgotten what it meant to see Mikkel lead his men. Being master of a ship seemed to come naturally to him. Filled with confidence, sure of what each man should do, Mikkel was not afraid to give orders and see that they were carried out.

As he stood at the tiller again, Mikkel looked like a young man who knew he was born to cross the oceans of the world. But now there was something more. His Christian commitment had given him a new wisdom—a source of help he hadn't known before.

On the way to Ireland, Devin started teaching Mikkel again. When someone else took the tiller, the two of them and Bree found a quiet place at the stern. To her surprise the lessons seemed to go longer and longer. It was as if her brother was trying to be sure that Mikkel had everything he needed to know.

The moments when the three of them talked together soon became special to Bree. After a while Devin started giving her and Mikkel a chance to talk with each other. Bree wondered about it. Then she thought she knew.

Soon the moment would come when they went their separate ways. More than likely, she and Devin would never see Mikkel again. With his deep, clear vision Devin was wise enough to know what needed to happen before then. Both she and Mikkel needed healing.

"I'll prove I'm worthy of trust," Mikkel had said.

"But how can I trust you when I wonder if you'll be honest?" Bree had asked years before. Did Mikkel even remember her words?

At times it tore her apart. One moment she believed in him. Trusted that he would do the right thing at the right time. The next moment she felt as if she was step-ping back, waiting. Always waiting.

Mikkel never told them what he planned. They only knew what he said long ago. "When I get to Ireland, I'll set things right."

Now he would have that opportunity. Would he talk to Brother Cronan, the monk at the Glendalough Monastery? As he taught Mikkel, Devin held the holy book that Cronan had used to bargain for the safety of his people. And what about the precious gems that Mikkel stole? Gems brought by pilgrims to the monastery?

But most of all, it was Mikkel's dark secret that concerned Bree. That secret would be easiest to hide. In all this time the three of them had never talked about Bjorn the cobbler and the silver coins Mikkel stole. Both Bree and Devin wanted him to make amends on his own—not because they forced him to be honest, but because it was the way he wanted to live.

Whenever Bree thought about it, she felt afraid for Mikkel. Afraid of his known thefts, but also of the hidden theft that could destroy his life. What would happen to Mikkel if he didn't act on what he said he believed?

It started Bree thinking. The time ahead would not be simple, and simple words would not be enough. Yet they must say something. When the moment came to say good-bye, how could she help Mikkel live with courage?

Then Bree realized that Thjodhild had given her the key. One day Bree asked, "Do you remember what Leif's mother said to you?"

Instantly, as though Mikkel had repeated the words a thousand times, he spoke. "The Lord Himself goes before you and will be with you."

Just as quickly Bree answered. "He will never leave you nor forsake you."

"Do not be afraid, Bree. Do not be discouraged."

They knew they were close to Ireland when they began seeing seabirds above them. As Mikkel sailed along the northern coast, they passed Rathlin. The waves washed against the shores, rising around the white rock at the base of the island.

Two days later, as they sailed down the east coast of Ireland, Devin stood next to Mikkel at the tiller. "Why don't you drop us off at Dublin?" Devin asked. "I'll show you where to sail in."

Mikkel faced him. "I know the way into Dublin," he said stiffly.

"Yes, I suppose you do," Devin answered just as stiffly.

"I'm going to stop in Dublin long enough to trade my goods and collect the earnings. Then I'll sail up the river at Arklow—"

"No!" Devin exclaimed. "You must not!"

"Don't you trust me?"

"That's not it. That's the way you came in before. You have a beard now. You're older. But if the men in our area find out who you are—"

"I know." Again Mikkel met his gaze.

Then Bree joined in. "Mikkel, please. Just drop us off. Dev and I will walk home from Dublin *or* Arklow."

When Mikkel turned to her, the expression in his

face softened. "Bree, on the day we met, you saved my life. When I learned that my men had captured you, I promised to watch out for you."

"And you have." Deep inside, Bree knew how true that was. "You truly have protected me, and I thank you. Now please watch out for yourself."

But Mikkel refused to listen. Fire in his eyes and standing tall, he lifted his head in the way Bree knew too well. "I, Mikkel, am son of Sigurd, mighty chieftain of the Aurland Fjord. You would dare to tell me what to do?"

Bree stared at him. She had almost forgotten how arrogant he could be. Her temper rising, she blurted out, "Yes, I would dare—"

When Mikkel grinned, she knew he was teasing, but Bree still felt a warning. "The danger is no joke," she said quietly.

Devin knew it too, for he said, "Mikkel, do you have any idea how a group of angry Irish might act?"

Mikkel laughed. "Probably not much different from a group of angry Vikings."

Then he grew serious again. "Bree, I took you from your parents. I will return you safely to your parents."

"No!" Bree exclaimed. "It's too dangerous!"

"I want to bring you home. To restore you to your father and mother. When I leave, I'll remember how you looked when you were with your family again."

As Bree looked into Mikkel's eyes, she saw a pain that went straight into his heart. When he lifted his head, Bree knew that he would not change his mind—not even if it cost him his life.

"First I must sail into Dublin and trade my goods," he said. When he grinned he looked like the old Mikkel. "I'm going to get a good return on all my time and hard work."

As the tides of the Irish Sea met the waters of the River Liffey, Devin spoke to Mikkel again. "Bree and I want to leave you at Dublin. For your safety, Mikkel."

But Mikkel didn't even turn from the tiller. "No, Dev. Don't ask me again."

An independent Norse kingdom, Dublin had been established by Vikings from the North Atlantic. It had become an important trade center. Like Mikkel's father, Devin and Bree's father, Aidan, often went there to trade.

On top of the high embankment around Dublin a tall fence of upright timbers gave added protection. As Mikkel's *Conquest* drew close to shore, his men took up oars and guided it in. Others leaped over the side and made the ship secure.

In a short time Mikkel gathered his goods and set out. Several men followed him, carrying what Mikkel wanted to trade. As soon as he thought it was safe, Devin followed Mikkel at a distance. Hours later, Devin was back.

"It was tough," he told Bree when he slipped back on board just ahead of Mikkel. "I followed him every step of the way. He seemed to know exactly where he was going. At each shop he bargained for a time and then left his goods. But he never went near Bjorn's street, let alone his cobbler's shop."

Sitting down on a keg, Devin leaned forward and supported his head in his hands. "Bree, I am so scared."

"He'll set things right," Bree whispered as Mikkel started up the ramp. "I know he will. I believe in him." But deep in her heart she, too, felt scared.

"Mikkel has changed," she said, trying to keep up her courage. "I know he's changed. You know it too."

But when Mikkel came over to talk with them he was filled with glee. "I've sold everything I wanted to sell. And I got top price for all of it! Didn't I tell you when we sailed to Greenland that I would become rich and famous?"

"Rich." Devin's voice was dark with disgust. "Not famous yet."

"I will be. You'll see."

"So what are you going to do, now that you have all this wealth?" Bree asked.

Instantly the carefree grin disappeared from Mikkel's face. "Put it to good use," he said quietly.

"And what use is that?"

Mikkel stared at her. "And what business is it of

yours? It's important that I trade well on this trip. Is that all right? Or do you want me to be a failure?"

Offended now, Bree stepped back. "My father is a trader. He taught us early to use honest weights."

"And you think I did not? So that's what this is about? Are you wondering if I'm a man of honor?"

"Bree—" Devin broke in, trying to warn her.

But Bree's disappointment welled up and spilled over. "I just want to know whether you were honest."

Suddenly the light went out of Mikkel's face. When he spoke, his words sounded as hard as stones. "Thanks, Bree. I thought you knew I had changed."

Turning, he stalked off the ship.

NINETEEN

IRISH SOIL

The dog Shadow returned to the ship after dark.

"That's not his name," Mikkel had said more than once.

"Yes, it is," Bree often answered. "He follows me around all the time." But judging by the look of him, Shadow must have covered all of Dublin.

His hair was always black, but now he was wet and dirty. When Bree scolded him, he sat down, looked up with beady eyes, and wagged his tail.

Bree sighed. If he wiggled close to her, she would be wet and dirty too.

Mikkel also returned after dark. The moment he came on board he told his men to lift the anchor. Soon they left the River Liffey and started once more down the east coast of Ireland.

Before long Bree and Devin began recognizing markers along the way. A headland—a high cliff that towered above the sea. A length of sandy beach. The huts of fishermen.

As the wind caught the great sail above them, Bree tried to feel glad. She was going home! For years she had wanted to know what lay beyond the Irish Sea. It had been her quest. But now that quest had changed. She simply wanted to be with her family again.

Mam and Daddy, her brother Adam, sisters Cara and Jen. And Keely who had been captured in an earlier Viking raid.

The distance between Bree and her family was growing less all the time. Soon she would be in the Wicklow Mountains. Soon she'd see Tully again. So why did she feel so upset?

Finally Bree had to be honest with herself. As much as she wanted to return home, she couldn't push aside her grief about Mikkel and his failure to talk with Bjorn. Both she and Devin felt unwilling to ask Mikkel about it. If their questions forced him to return the stolen coins, it would never be the same as if he'd freely done it himself.

But something else also bothered Bree. When she was desperate for God's help, He had called her to be a light in the places where she was taken as a slave. Without knowing that, Mikkel even said that she was a light wherever she was. But would Tully understand how she had changed? By now he seemed like a fuzzy faraway person who wasn't real.

Before first light, Mikkel anchored the *Conquest* in a quiet cove. Tucked out of sight, they waited through the day.

Mikkel talked first with Nola. "I want to make amends for what I did."

But Nola stopped him. "Thank you, Mikkel. You already have. I can see the change in you. God took what you did and used it for good." Drawing close to Garth, she circled his arm with her hands.

"I want to visit my family," Nola said. "To see if my mother is still alive. If she is, I want her to meet Garth and know what a special husband I have. Then I want to go back to the Aurland Fjord. My home is with Garth."

With waves lapping around the ship and sunlight upon the water, Mikkel spoke to Bree. "When you step down on Irish soil I want you to know that you are free."

Unable to speak, Bree looked up into his face. Where was the anger she had seen only last night? Somehow Mikkel had put it aside. Now he gathered together the Irish among them.

Nola, two men who worked on his crew, Devin, and Bree. Standing in the bow, Mikkel spoke in a clear voice that carried to everyone on his ship.

"Briana, I give you your freedom. I set you free, as you

were always meant to be. I wish you great happiness and that your heart will come home."

Drawing a deep breath, Bree looked to the shore. The countless shades of Irish green seemed to reach out to her. Yes! It had finally happened.

Then her gaze returned to Mikkel. As her eyes grew wet she said, "With all my heart I receive my freedom."

Though Arklow was a Viking settlement, Mikkel waited until after dark before bringing the *Conquest* into the river. Without a sound, his oarsmen rowed past the dark cottages and sleeping people.

Farther upstream they drew into shore. Working quietly, the men lifted the deck boards and threw out the rocks used as ballast to keep the ship stable. When they put out into the river again, the ship rode higher, drawing less water.

Mikkel guided the ship as far upriver as they could go. Then as Bree and Devin stood beside him, he spoke quietly. "Are you ready to go? Nola and Garth too?"

Gathering up her one small bag of belongings, Bree closed the top. Inside, where no one could see, was the birch bark basket from Hóp. And inside the basket, the dried blue flower still lay protected within a nest of soft cloths.

Strange, Bree thought. *I left with nothing but the clothes on my back. I return much the same way.*

Then she knew. She returned with five years filled with memories. Some bad memories, but many more that were good.

I return, knowing that I'm a different person. Knowing that You, God, have been faithful to me.

Standing before Mikkel, Bree held out the woven basket from Nikmaq. "Will you give this to your mother? She'll like the beautiful weaving. And tell her thanks for the sea chest she gave me. Tell her it kept my clothes dry and helped me stay warm."

"Take it with you," he said. "I'll help you carry it."

"Oh, no. It's for sailing, being at sea."

"You can use it as a bench. A chest of memories. When you look at it, remember—" Suddenly Mikkel turned away.

When the *Conquest* drew close to shore, he picked up Bree's sea chest, lifted it to his shoulder, and carried it off the ship. In the soft darkness of night he turned back and helped her down the ramp.

"Remember," he said softly. "When you step onto Irish soil, you are free."

Bree swallowed around the lump in her throat. "Thank you, Mikkel," she whispered. "Thank you."

Under one arm he carried a sealskin package and Bree knew what it was—the book from the monastery. Maybe Mikkel was going there. Maybe he would talk with Brother Cronan. It gave her hope.

"All right if I put this inside the chest?" Mikkel asked. "It'll be easier to carry."

Bree nodded, but still clung to her bag. She didn't want anything to happen to the dried flower.

When they started walking, Shadow leaped over the side. Kneeling down, Bree scratched behind his ears and stroked his back one last time. Then Bree pointed to the ship. "Go back," she commanded in her strongest whisper.

The dog sat down on his haunches, looked at her, and tipped his head as though listening. But he would not move.

Again Bree pointed to the ship. When he stayed exactly where he was, Bree turned to Mikkel. "You tell him."

But Mikkel said, "Take Shadow along. He's become your dog."

Bree shook her head. "He's yours." Much as she wanted to keep him, she knew that Shadow would always remind her of Mikkel. "Go on, Shadow. Go back."

Instead, the dog wiggled forward on his belly until he was halfway between them. There he lay, looking first at one, then the other.

"He'll give you away," Bree said, afraid now for Mikkel.

"No, he won't." Hoisting Bree's sea chest onto his shoulder again, Mikkel set out.

But Shadow whimpered. Finally Bree whispered to him, "All right, come along."

She had taken only five steps when she noticed that Hammer followed too. At first Bree thought he was walking with Nola and Garth. Then, after a time, Bree and Nola gave each other a long good-bye hug. Nola and Garth took one direction while Bree, Devin, Mikkel, and Hammer took another.

The way was long, and at the end, the path was steeply uphill. To Bree's surprise, Hammer insisted that he go with them. He even made a joke of it.

"I'm your bodyguard," he told Mikkel. "I'll watch your back." But Bree knew that Hammer probably spoke truth.

Just the same, he showed an understanding for what was happening that Bree didn't expect. Though staying close by, he dropped far enough back so that she and Mikkel and Devin could talk without feeling he was listening.

As the sun rose over the land, they walked deeper into the forest and stayed away from well-traveled paths. Each time Bree recognized something she knew she spoke of it. When they passed a cottage or farm, she always asked about those who lived there.

Finally Devin said, "Don't forget, Bree. Anything I know about the people is over three years old."

With a quick glance at Mikkel, Bree fell silent. But Devin turned to him as though finishing a conversation. "Remember what I said about Bree?"

For an instant a question flicked through Mikkel's eyes, then was gone.

"Remember our agreement?" Devin asked.

Mikkel nodded.

"When we reach the door of our house, my father is the one who knows what's best for Bree."

Again Mikkel nodded, as though understanding what Devin did not say.

As Bree, Devin, Mikkel, and Hammer walked through the forest, they came to the river and the stepping-stones that led to the O'Toole farm. Beyond lay the gate set in a stone wall. A high earthen mound or rampart joined the stone, making a large, circular enclosure around the buildings. A fence of tall, closely set timbers topped the earthen wall.

A deep circular trench lay inside the enclosure. The clay from digging that trench had been thrown up on the inside, making the wall. Shaped and faced, it formed the high mound of protection, a ring fort.

The water in the river was low, and Bree stopped, looking across through the open gate. From where she stood she could see the house where she had longed to be all these years. Smoke curled up from the hole in the roof, seeming to welcome her.

Home, Bree thought. *Home*.

"I'm scared, Dev," she said.

"Keely felt the same way when she came back. She even asked, 'Will Mam and Daddy still love me?'"

"What if they've changed? What if something has happened to them? I want them to be like I remember them. Strong and—"

Again Bree glanced at Mikkel. He had turned away, and Bree knew she was hurting him.

Holding her skirt above the water, she started across the stepping-stones. From one stone to another she leaped with the ease of long practice. When she reached the other side, Mikkel and Devin were close behind.

"I'll stay here," Hammer said from across the river. Just inside the tree line he sat down to wait where he could not be easily seen.

When Bree passed through the gate there was no stopping her. As swift as a deer she ran with the ease of knowing what it meant to run with the wind. When she reached the house the top half of the door was open. Leaning over the closed bottom, Bree peered in.

"Anyone home?"

"Anyone home?" It was Mam who answered. "It's you? Bree?"

In an instant Mam was outside. Throwing her arms around Bree, she hugged her as if she would never let her go. Still holding each other tightly, they began sobbing and neither of them could stop.

In that moment Aidan O'Toole appeared in the door-way. One of the dark Irish, he stood tall with his black mane of hair nearly touching the doorway. "What's this? *Bree?*"

Coming outside, he threw his long arms around Bree and her mother. Then he whirled both of them around and around until everyone laughed and cried at the same time.

Suddenly Aidan stopped and stood still, facing Bree. "Welcome home, my daughter," he said softly.

"Home," Bree answered softly, barely able to believe it had really happened. It still felt strange, so odd, so—

Gently her daddy reached out and tipped up her chin until she looked into his eyes. "Home is where the heart is," he said. "My heart has been with you wherever you've been."

Bree blinked. How could her father always understand? "And my heart has been here," she answered. "With you, and Mam, and Adam, and Cara, and Jen, and Keely. My heart has been here in the long days and the long nights—"

In that moment Bree remembered Mikkel. He stood with Devin off to one side, waiting. "Daddy, this is Mikkel. He was master of the ship—"

As Mikkel stepped forward, he bowed, then faced Bree's father. "I wanted to bring Bree home to you."

Aidan looked stunned. "*You* are Mikkel?"

Though Aidan was tall, the two stood eye to eye. As a chieftain who measured each man he met, Aidan studied Mikkel's face.

Watching, Bree tried to see Mikkel as her father would. The wind and summer sun had made his flyaway hair even blonder, but his beard was slightly darker. He wore long, narrow trousers and a red, finely sewn tunic with laced cuffs. With his ornamented sword in its sheath, he stood straight and tall with shoulders back and feet apart, as though ready for battle if needed.

Yet it was Mikkel's eyes that told Bree most. His face held a respect for her father that startled her.

As tears slid down Mam's cheeks, Aidan spoke again. "Somehow I didn't expect you—" Aidan stopped, as though knowing that anything he said could be misunderstood.

"To be like I am?"

Aidan nodded.

"I wasn't this way once—"

Bree broke in. "He was arrogant and terrible."

But Aidan didn't even look at Bree. He was watching Mikkel. "And now?" Aidan asked.

Again Mikkel bowed low, first to Bree's mother, then to her father. "I am deeply sorry for the sorrow I have caused you. I ask your forgiveness."

Again Aidan looked stunned, as if he could not take it in. "You came from your far north country to bring Bree home?"

"Actually from a new world beyond Iceland and Greenland."

"You really came to bring Bree home?" Mam asked.

She, too, looked as if she couldn't believe what she was hearing.

"I needed to keep a promise." Mikkel glanced toward Devin and Bree. "A pledge to bring both of them here. And I wanted to be sure Bree reached you safely."

"But what has changed you?" Aidan asked. "You don't seem like the kind of person who would lead a raid."

Again Mikkel glanced over to Bree and Devin, then faced their father. "They told me about the God that you serve. I have asked your God—your Jesus—to forgive me."

Suddenly Aidan put his arm around his wife. As if they were one person, they moved toward Mikkel. "It's what we prayed for," Aidan said as he offered his hand.

"We asked God to make Bree a light to the nations." Mam's voice quavered, then grew strong.

As Mikkel took her hand, Aidan put both of his hands around theirs. "We forgive you, Mikkel," he said. "Our family forgives you. We welcome you into our home."

But Mikkel stood with disbelief in his eyes. From one to the other he looked, as though unable to understand what he heard. "You ask me into your home? Just like that? How can you possibly forgive me?"

Reaching out, Aidan drew Bree and Devin close, but spoke to Mikkel. "When someone you love goes out the door and does not come back, your life is forever changed.

If we had not forgiven you, we would not have been able to go on. And when I look at Bree, I know that you truly did keep her safe."

When Mikkel's shoulders trembled, one tear, then another, ran down his cheeks. As tears welled up in Bree's eyes, Devin put one arm around her and the other around Mikkel. But it was their parents who drew them into a circle. As the five of them stood together, their arms tightened as if they would never let one person go.

At last Mikkel drew a long breath and wiped his eyes. "I need to leave," he said. But Aidan answered, "Come. It's time to eat."

As the others went into the house, Mikkel faced Bree. "Your father is a chieftain. I've been around enough leaders to know. You never told me."

When Bree didn't answer, he said, "You thought I would raise the ransom. Well, yes, I probably would have done that too."

When Bree still didn't say a word, he searched her face. "That's why you weren't afraid to ask if you could go to a monastery school. That's why—"

But Bree shook her head, stopping him. "It's all right, Mikkel. Even though I was a slave you protected me and treated me with respect. Isn't that what's important?"

Soon after they went inside, Bree's sister Keely came in. The moment she saw Bree, Keely burst into tears.

"I've always had a scared spot right here," she said, laying her hands over her heart. "Ever since you gave me your chance to go home, I've wondered if you would be able to come back."

As they were eating, Adam returned, took one look at his sister, and said, "Bree? You're home?"

Five years older and much taller, Adam had grown up while she was gone. At twelve he still wore the same I-will-protect-my-sister look. He, too, hugged Bree until she nearly lost her breath.

But then Adam stood back, looked at Mikkel and told him, "You took my sister away."

"I'm sorry," Mikkel said.

"That's not enough!" Adam glared at him.

As if they didn't quite know what to do with Bree, nine-year-old Cara and eight-year-old Jen stood behind Adam. At first they just watched her. Then when Bree talked to them, they remembered her voice and flew into her arms.

The look in their eyes told Bree that Mikkel truly was in trouble. Though Keely knew him from Norway, she also stood quietly, saying nothing, as if waiting for her father to speak.

"We have forgiven Mikkel," he told the children. "Your mam and I expect you to forgive him too."

But each time Adam looked at Mikkel a cold stillness settled in his face.

TWENTY

THE SAME PERSON?

"You've become a beautiful young woman," her mother told Bree as they cleaned up after the midday meal. "There's a new softness in your eyes."

Her mother's words surprised Bree. She had not had much time to think about growing up. She had only grieved that she would be past the usual age to wed.

"You're not only beautiful on the outside," Mam went on. "It's as though a shining light comes through you."

Trying to hide how much the words meant to her, Bree set down the cup she was wiping. But her mother asked, "It's because you've suffered, isn't it?"

As often before, Bree felt surprised by the depth of

Mam's understanding. "Not physically," Bree said. "But in my heart, and mind, and spirit."

Bree didn't want to tell her mother what it was like to be a slave. To work hard, yes, but she had always done that. Instead, to be told where she must go and what she must do, and what she could not do. To have boundaries around her that seemed like stone walls. From a young age Bree had known how to make good choices. Slavery meant she was not allowed to make choices.

Most difficult of all was not having the freedom to walk wherever she wanted and climb the mountains whenever she chose. Growing up in the Wicklow Mountains, she had learned to climb with the skill of a mountain goat. But worst of all, she had not had the freedom to be the person God meant her to be. Not at first.

"I learned something," Bree said. "No matter how often someone said I was a slave, I was not. I am a daughter of my powerful God. Because of that, I was more free than those who called me a slave."

Picking up a bowl, Bree wiped and set it away. Strange how much she had gone through in learning to live again.

Now Mam was curious. "Mikkel's parents? What are they like?"

"Norwegian, of course." Bree smiled. "When Mikkel's mother welcomed him home, he was late. For some time his mother had wondered if he, too, had gone down in the sea. Yet when she saw Mikkel, only one tear slid down her cheek."

"'He, too'?"

"Like his oldest brother, Ivar. Mikkel's father, Sigurd, is a chieftain like Daddy. Tall, and strong, and wise. His people respect him. He wanted Mikkel to be a merchant, not a raider. He was upset when he learned about Mikkel's raid and that he had taken Irish as prisoners. He told Mikkel, 'Unless you find a way to set your actions right, you'll be a slave to what you have done.'"

"Mikkel." When Mam said his name she watched Bree carefully. "Doesn't he understand the danger in coming back?"

Though he didn't speak of it, Bree felt sure that Mikkel knew. "He said it was something he must do. When he learned that his men had brought me onto the ship, I reminded him that I had saved his life."

Mam's eyes held her laughter. "You spit it out, you mean. You told him he owed you something."

Bree laughed. Her mother knew her well. "Mikkel wouldn't let me go, but he promised to take care of me. And he has."

"First, it was his men who captured you? Then Mikkel promised to watch out for you?"

Mam started to laugh, but to Bree it wasn't funny. Instead, tears welled up in her eyes. She had spent so much time hating Mikkel that now she couldn't understand why she felt the way she did.

"But with Mikkel it's more than that, isn't it? More than just watching out for you?"

Though five years had passed, Bree's mother had not changed. Well, maybe, one little bit. She had grown even stronger.

"Devin wants me to marry an Irish lad," Bree said. "All these years I've wanted to see what Tully has become."

Suddenly her mother turned away. As Mam hung the towels near the cooking fire to dry, Bree wondered about it. *What's wrong?*

The back of her mother's head gave Bree no understanding. What did her mother know that she didn't?

When Tully appeared at the door he gave Devin a big grin and an arm wrestle. But then Tully looked beyond Devin to Mikkel.

"C'mon, Mikkel, let's go for a walk," Devin said quickly as he headed for the door. "We'll take the path along the upper lake," he told Bree, as though warning her to go in another direction.

As Bree looked at Tully, it startled her. She had forgotten how much he looked like Mikkel. In the moment that Tully stood before her, Bree felt a shock run down her spine, as if he shouldn't look that way.

"Welcome home, Bree," he said. His smile was warm and welcoming, as though there had been no five years between.

But Bree felt shy before him. After walking through most of the night and then the morning, she had barely had time to comb her long, wavy hair. She wished she had been able to clean up, change clothes, look her best.

Then Tully grinned, and it was like old times. "You've grown up, Bree. You're beautiful."

They walked through the forest to the wide spot in the river where Bree used to watch her younger sisters and brother swim. Below that place, she and Tully sat down on the grassy bank of the river.

At first they could barely talk fast enough, using the Irish both of them had known since earliest memory. "Remember?" Tully often said, and they laughed at something that happened when they were children.

Tully still knew the things that struck her funny. Bree still remembered how to make him laugh. Each of them had their own special memories. It seemed that Tully could recall every time their two families had been together.

As much as she thought she knew him, Bree was learning new things about Tully. At last she understood. He remembered all this because he had often thought about them.

Then he asked, "How are you doing, Bree? How are

you *really* doing?" And she knew Tully honestly wanted to know.

She started by telling him where she had been and what she had seen. Leaving out the hard spots, she instead told the best.

"And Mikkel?" he asked finally. "It was Mikkel who helped you see all this?"

"Mikkel?" Bree stopped midsentence. "What does he have to do with it?"

"He showed you the world."

Bree stared at Tully. "I didn't *want* to be captured, to be taken away as a slave—"

"I know. But you saw the world—Mikkel's country, Iceland, Greenland, even a new world."

"Yes," Bree said quietly. The lump in her throat was growing larger. So large in fact that she could barely swallow. This wasn't how she expected her homecoming to be.

But then Tully said, "You've changed, Bree."

"You, too, Tully."

But he shook his head, met her gaze squarely. "Not the way you have. You've learned so much that I don't know. You've seen so much that I haven't."

"Not because I wanted to," Bree was quick to point out. "Because I had no choice. I wanted to be here."

Then she saw Tully look toward the stepping-stones across the river. The stones where Mikkel had fallen on that day five years ago. Suddenly Bree wished they weren't sitting so close to the place where she met Mikkel. Bree pushed the thought away, feeling grateful that she was with Tully instead. Tully was safe.

Tully was Tully.

"Bree, there's something I don't understand. You were a slave, but you seem free. You had to travel dangerous waters, yet you seemed to like it. Weren't you upset? Weren't you afraid?"

Bree stared at him. Of all the things she had expected, it wasn't this. "Tully, don't you understand? That's why I've changed."

Starting at the beginning, Bree told him what she had been forced to learn along the way. "I didn't like what was happening to me," she said. "In fact, I told God quite often that I hated it."

Finally Bree tried to describe what had upset her most. "Because I saved Mikkel from drowning he was able to lead the raid. Besides taking Dev and me away from our home, he took your cousin Lil and separated so many other families."

When Bree finished, she and Tully were quiet for a long time.

"Dev told me," Tully said at last. "When Mikkel fell and hit his head, you thought it was me."

Bree nodded. Even now when she thought of that terrible moment she could barely speak. When she could not find any words, Tully looked again at the stepping-stones.

When he turned back to her, Bree was still watching him.

"All this time——"

"I know," Bree answered. "Me too. I kept thinking about you because I knew that you were strong, and true, and faithful, wanting the best for everyone you know. I needed to remember that when days were hard."

"But not anymore?"

"There was something I learned," Bree said slowly. Inside, she felt relieved that at last they seemed able to talk about what was most important. But a tight knot in her stomach warned her that she wasn't going to like where their talking would end.

Afraid now, she started guarding her words. If they waited for another day, it could be like old times again. If she could just get cleaned up and put on a new dress—a dress in the bright blue she loved instead of the undyed wool worn by a slave. If she wore such a dress she would feel better—like a neighbor and friend.

"Finally there was something I knew," Bree said. "No matter how awful something is—even when I don't think I'm going to get through—if I ask God to help me in whatever I face, He'll give me the courage to win."

Once more Bree glanced toward the stepping-stones. Then she faced Tully again. "I'm still the same person——"

Suddenly Bree broke off. She wasn't the same person. Not anymore.

IF YOU VALUE YOUR LIFE—

When he and Devin set out, Mikkel wasn't surprised that his friend took an upper path. High on the mountainside there were fewer people. Here, possibly, they would see no one.

They had walked for a time when Mikkel stopped to look out from between the trees. Far below lay the high stone walls of the Glendalough Monastery. From this height he could see the entire monastic city at once. A large stone church, other smaller churches and buildings. Small huts and larger dwelling places, all with their thatched straw roofs. Sheep, cattle, horses, geese. Gardens and fields of grain. Everything that was needed for daily life. And with it, people.

Some on pilgrimage, standing before a high cross. Men in brown robes going about their daily work, as if no one could hurt them. But he had. In spite of the biggest barrier of all—a stone tower almost one hundred feet high, he had hurt them.

As though it had been yesterday instead of five years ago, Mikkel remembered. He had spent part of a day and a night on the side of this mountain, learning the lay of the land. Dangerous as it was to walk unknown heights, the dark held no fear for him. Instead, as the first light had crept across the forested slopes, Mikkel knew he had the information he needed.

He had spied out the land and could give his men an accurate report. From high above he had found the best way to get in. Already he had formed his plan of attack.

"Mikkel?" Devin asked, bringing him back to the present.

Mikkel shifted the sealskin package under one arm. "I need to go alone from here."

"I want to go with you," Devin replied.

Mikkel shook his head. "This is something I have to do for myself."

"You remember the way?"

"I remember the way."

Mikkel set off at once before Devin could say more. Then at a turn in the path, Mikkel stopped and looked back. "Thanks, Dev, for everything."

It sounded like a good-bye, and Mikkel knew it could become that.

A short distance farther on, he left the path and started dropping down the mountainside. When he reached the river, he crossed over on stepping-stones. Ahead of him were the high stone walls that surrounded the monastery.

The gate was open and through the archway Mikkel saw a second archway. Stones and timbers between them supported a small house over the entrance. A man in a long brown robe stood next to the heavy wooden doors.

When the monk who was the gatekeeper spoke to him, Mikkel asked to talk with Brother Cronan. The keeper searched Mikkel's face and seemed to like what he saw.

"He'll be working now," the monk said. Standing aside, he pointed to the path along an inside wall. "Take the first turning. Look for a building where several men work. You'll find Brother Cronan in an inner room where he copies the holy words."

But Mikkel looked up at the thick stone walls. On his right, and just inside the entryway, the outline of a cross was cut into a massive slab of rock. When Mikkel stopped before it, the gatekeeper spoke again.

"For a place of refuge it is. If a man flees danger—if someone wants to take his life to get even for what he did —such a man can come to the cross and receive protection."

In that moment Mikkel grew still. Standing there, he

stared at the cross, but the monk's words fell around him. "Sometimes a man comes to us only minutes ahead of those who would kill him. The man needing refuge runs to the stone, touches the cross—"

"And he is safe?" Mikkel spoke through stiff lips.

"We give him sanctuary."

"Sanctuary?"

"Refuge. Safety. Protection. As long as he is here, we protect him from those who hate him. We offer the Lord's peace."

For a moment longer Mikkel stood there. Unable to move on, he reached out, traced the deeply cut mark of the cross with his fingers.

Sanctuary. Protection. Peace.

Will I ever truly know peace? Or will the haunting guilt of what I did be with me the rest of my life?

"Is something wrong?" the monk asked.

Mikkel shook his head. Then, as he started away, he spoke. "Something is finally right." For now he knew what he must say to Brother Cronan.

Shifting his sealskin package, Mikkel went on. In a few steps he came to another cross, this time a high granite one. Suddenly the surprise of it struck Mikkel. The first time he was here he had no idea what a cross meant.

A large stone church lay nearby. A *cathedral*. Mikkel had heard the word and decided that must be what this was.

As he followed the path again, he looked up to the cone-shaped stone tower. Close at hand, its nearly one-hundred-foot height seemed even more remarkable.

A bell tower? Perhaps. But right from the beginning Mikkel had felt it was more.

From high on the mountain he had studied the tower enough to know that anyone who looked out the windows at the top could see in every direction. And the entry was more than thirteen feet off the ground—high enough to require a ladder that could be pulled up when everyone was safely inside.

This he had known, and Mikkel had expected all the people and treasures to be here. Had the tower been built to resist a raider like him? To say, "We are standing strong in our faith, in spite of everyone and everything that comes against it"?

If so, the tower hadn't been enough. Instead, one man had done just that. Because Brother Cronan stood against him when he came to steal, Mikkel was here now—a changed person.

Mikkel found the monk sitting on a high stool inside a stone building. Brother Cronan's long hair fell away from the shaved part of his head. His brown robe hung to the floor around his sandaled feet. With a steady pen he wrote on the vellum, or calfskin, that was used for honored books such as the Bible.

Though five years and thousands of miles had passed

between them, Mikkel instantly recognized the monk. On that day when Mikkel led the raid, he had found Brother Cronan hiding the large book with a white cover and precious gems. The monk had used it to bargain for the lives of his people.

How could he stand at sword point with such courage? How could anyone show so little fear? But Brother Cronan seemed to have no concern for his own life—only for that of others.

Now, afraid that he would startle the monk and cause him to make a mistake, Mikkel waited. When Cronan laid down his pen, he turned to face Mikkel. "Ahhh, you are back."

"You remember me?"

"How could I forget?" Cronan searched his face. "You have changed."

"I came to return your holy book." With great care Mikkel set the sealskin package on a nearby table.

"I came to return your precious gems." Reaching inside his tunic, Mikkel took out a leather bag and set it next to the book of the four Gospels.

"I came to offer a gift because I'm sorry for all I took from you." Taking out another bag, he set it beside the first.

As Cronan waited, Mikkel looked into his eyes. "And I have come to ask your forgiveness."

Swallowing hard, Mikkel tried to speak, but could not go on. Again the monk waited.

At last Mikkel said, "I am sorry for what I did to you. I'm sorry for what I did to the Irish people."

"Yes."

"Taking them from their homes. Making them captives, slaves. Taking them away from their families—"

Again Mikkel stopped. When at last he spoke, his voice broke again. "Away from their loved ones. Separating families forever."

Covering his face with his hands, Mikkel began to weep. Dropping down, he knelt with his face to the stone floor. His shoulders shook as he wept until he could weep no more. Only then did Brother Cronan speak.

"In the name of our Lord I forgive you," he said. "On behalf of all the people you have wronged, I forgive you."

Startled, Mikkel looked up. Though Bree and Devin had forgiven him countless times, how could Brother Cronan forgive him on behalf of everyone he had hurt?

It stunned Mikkel. For five long years he had carried the weight of what he had done. Now with Brother Cronan's words, that weight was gone.

"But how can I ever make things right?"

"You can't. Oh, you can try. You can ask about the Irish slaves who want to come home. But the lives of people you captured won't ever be what they would have been. Still—"

Brother Cronan thought about it. "You can ask God to bring great blessing out of the wrong you have done."

"Great blessing? How can there possibly be great blessing when I've hurt so many people?"

Cronan smiled. "If you decide to try it, you'll find out."

Going to the table, he unwrapped the package. "Ahhh, safely home. I sent it on a long journey. Thank you for bringing it back. Did it help?"

Mikkel nodded. "Dev and Bree used it to teach me—"

"And have they taught you about the apostle Paul? The one named Saul who brought trouble upon God's people?"

Mikkel grinned. "Most certainly. Once Dev knew I would listen, he wasted no time in telling me the story."

Cronan laughed. "And Bree? I suspect Bree hasn't changed terribly much."

Mikkel met his eyes. "I think that in some ways Bree has changed more than any of us will ever know."

Before leaving, Mikkel had one more question. "Would you be willing to send another one of your books on a journey? Do you have a copy without precious gems? I can't read Latin, but maybe Bree or Dev could teach me."

Suddenly Mikkel paused, remembering. There would be no more time for that.

But Cronan said, "As soon as possible, I'll have a copy of the New Testament ready."

As Mikkel started for the door, Cronan warned him. "Watch yourself, Mikkel. If you value your life, you must leave Wicklow at once."

TWENTY-TWO

STANDING WATCH

W hen Bree saw Mikkel return to the house she wondered where he had been. But Devin asked no questions. He seemed to know. Instead, it was their father who asked Mikkel question after question about his life. Bree knew her father well enough to know that in countless ways he was learning who Mikkel was and what he believed.

As they sat down to the evening meal, Aidan's questions continued. Where had Mikkel traveled? How did he like being a merchant? Did he often bring his goods to the Dublin trade center? With each question Mikkel answered with the respect he gave his own father and Leif Erikson.

Mikkel and Aidan were still talking when Bree and her mother cleaned up after the evening meal. Bree had worked with her mother for so long that she still knew where everything was. When they bumped into each other in a small space they laughed as they had when Bree was a child.

The warmth of being home flooded her heart. Yet so much had happened during the five years. To Bree it seemed only yesterday since she worked with Mikkel's mother. Rika had taught her to use a Norse loom and weave the cloth that became the sail in Mikkel's ship. Rika and Mikkel's grandmother had been kind to her.

Now Bree missed her own grandmother, who had died while she was gone. But then she told Mam how Mikkel's mother protected her.

"You've been cared for, haven't you?" Mam asked.

"By Leif Erikson's mother. And by Mikkel's mother, Rika."

She had forgotten how her mother always saw more than Bree expected. "It was strange," she said. "As we worked together we became friends."

"It *is* strange," her mother answered. "But I can understand it. What is Mikkel's mother like?"

"Strong. Strong like you. You don't look alike. She's tall and blonde. Her eyes are blue instead of the brown eyes you and I have. With both of us our hair is more reddish blonde. But you and Mikkel's mother are both strong inside. At first I didn't understand Rika because she hid her emotions, even when something really dreadful happened."

Mam smiled. "Not like the Irish."

Bree grinned. "Not like the Irish. But when we sailed out of the fjord I looked back and wondered if I'd ever see her again."

A shadow entered Mam's eyes. "Do you think you will?"

"I don't know." Bree changed the subject. "It's so good to be home!"

Filled with gladness at being together again, Bree threw her arms around her mother. "We'll have to keep hugging each other until we finally catch up." But when Bree set the wooden bowls on a shelf she still saw the shadow in Mam's eyes.

When Tully's cousin Lil came to the house she surrounded Bree with hugs. Lil's words spilled over so fast that she could barely get them out. Both of them knew what it meant to be slaves because of Mikkel's raid. Yet when Bree could have gained her freedom, she gave that opportunity to Lil. Bree wanted the younger girl to return home.

As Devin edged his way into their conversation, Bree smiled. It wasn't difficult to see that Lil was also eager to talk with him.

Suddenly Bree remembered Hammer. "On the edge of the woods there's a man standing watch," she told her mother. "He wants to protect Mikkel. I need to bring him food."

Outside, Shadow ran up to her. Quickly Bree fed him, then told him to stay where he was. This time he obeyed.

In that not-quite-dark moment, faraway trees on the top of a mountain stood black against a lighter sky. From the nearby slopes, Bree heard water falling from one level to the next. Then partway up the mountain, above the earth-and-timber wall that surrounded the house, she sensed a quick movement.

At first Bree wondered if she had imagined a stirring of wind in the trees. Or was there someone looking down at her from above? If so, would he be able to tell that she was watching for any sign that he was there?

Kneeling down, Bree acted as if she was talking to Shadow. While she scratched behind his ears, she watched everything around her.

In the high wall of the ring fort the gate was closed now. Her father had taken the precaution of having men stand next to it. But what was happening on the forested slopes outside the wall?

Bree waited. This time the movement was lower on the mountain but still above the wall where she could see it. Then a second shadow moved. Someone running from tree to tree. The soft earth and flowing water hid the sound, but the trunk of the second tree looked thicker than before.

A warning shiver ran down Bree's spine. A moment later a third shadow followed the second. Then suddenly the night was full of dark figures creeping from one place to the next. Not one, not two, not even three, but many people hid in the forest on the mountain near their home.

Her muscles tense with fear, Bree stayed low, as if talking to the dog. The openness of the area around the door made her uneasy. Still on her knees, she moved slowly to a nearby bush. How could she make it look as if she didn't know what was happening?

Just then Keely opened the door and came out. In that moment a man appeared behind the bush next to Bree. Startled, she gasped.

"Shhh!" he warned, and Bree knew it was Hammer. True to his word he had stood watch.

"Mikkel told your father about me," Hammer said. "He told the men at the gate to let me in. Do you see what's happening? Mikkel needs to flee."

"How do you know?" Bree whispered.

"I listened. I heard what they said."

"Meet us at the edge of the forest," Bree answered. "At the stepping-stones downstream from the crossing by the gate."

As Hammer disappeared into the darkness, Bree waited. When Cara and Jen came outside, Bree decided it was the best she could hope for. Standing up, she walked toward them as if nothing was happening and slipped back into the house. She headed straight for her father.

Aidan took one look at her face and spoke in a low voice. "What's wrong?"

"Men are gathering outside."

"Angry men?"

"They're slipping from one tree to the next, as though trying to hide what they're doing. How do they know Mikkel is here? From Tully?"

"I don't think so. I asked Tully not to say anything, but—"

Not Tully. Bree felt relieved. Yet her father's face looked grim. "But what?" she asked.

"Lil says your brother Adam told the neighborhood. He was proud of himself, as though he had become the protector of our family."

Bree swallowed hard. The knot in her stomach had moved up to become a lump in her throat. The Irish had every right to be angry. Some had lost children to the raid, others a brother, or sister, or parent. Now the leader of the Vikings who took them away stood within their reach.

"Mikkel can't go to his ship," Aidan said. "The way there will be watched. Take him to the monastery."

Bree thought quickly. "If he reaches the sanctuary stone—if I can get him there—"

"When you were gone, we changed the hiding place."

Bree wasn't surprised. Years ago she had known her

father thought the small underground cellar was inadequate for hiding women and children. That was the reason he had built the shelter in the forest.

"The underground passageway is longer and goes under the earth wall. You'll come out in the meadow next to trees that can hide you until it's safe to move on."

"And you want me to take Mikkel that way?" It startled Bree. Without doubt it had taken great effort to build a tunnel. How could Daddy show such a valuable secret to the person who had been his enemy?

But her father simply said, "I trust him now. Dev and I will talk to the men. Maybe they won't notice you're gone. But don't take any chances. An angry mob——"

When Bree looked around she saw Mikkel watching. His eyes wary, as if he understood what had happened, Mikkel stood up and started toward them. As he passed the bench where Devin sat, Mikkel dropped his hand on his shoulder. Leaning down, Mikkel spoke quietly.

"If I never see you again, I want you to know that you have made me rich by becoming my friend."

When Devin started to stand, he glanced around and sat down again. Reaching up, he clasped Mikkel's hand.

"I wish it could have been different," Devin said just as quietly. "Courage to win, Mikkel."

"Courage to win, Dev."

"I'll never forget you. I'll never stop praying for you."

When Mikkel turned toward him, Aidan stood up.

As if nothing important was happening, he headed toward the end of the house farthest from the door. A row of small enclosures with partitions that went partway to the ceiling hid that end of the house from the people next to the fire.

Each enclosure was big enough for one bed, but Aidan walked to a small area beyond them. There he picked up a small low table and set it down nearby. When he pushed aside the rushes on the dirt floor, Bree saw a trapdoor.

Without making a sound, her father lifted the wooden door. After propping it against the wall, he cupped Bree's face between his hands.

"God go with you, child," he said. "I pray that you will always know that home is where the heart is."

Startled, Bree met his gaze. "What do you mean?" she whispered.

"When you need to understand you will."

Quickly he lit a candle, handed it to Bree, and then turned to Mikkel. "Bree knows the forest even better than Devin. I've told her to take you to the monastery."

"But—"

"The trapdoor at the end of the passageway will be heavy to lift. When you climb out and close the door just be sure the turf goes back in place. Hurry now—"

Yet Mikkel waited. "I don't want to be a danger for you and Bree and your family."

Aidan shook his head. "I respect you for the changes in your life."

In the dim light Bree saw Mikkel's face. The shock in his eyes. The disbelief. The light of gratitude. Then he spoke. "I cannot thank you enough."

Aidan stretched out a hand, then circled Mikkel's shoulders instead. "Thank you for bringing my daughter safely home."

As Bree started down the ladder into the passageway, she felt the dampness. Reaching the bottom, she held out the light and Mikkel followed her. When his feet touched the ground of the cellar, the trapdoor above them closed without sound. In the flickering light of the candle they waited until their eyes were used to the darkness.

"What's out there?" Mikkel whispered.

"Men." Bree barely breathed the word. "A lot of them, I think. I couldn't tell for sure."

"A mob?"

"Probably."

Mikkel took her arm. "Stay here, Bree. I don't want you hurt."

"Daddy told me to help you get away. He wants to protect you."

The surprise of it caught Mikkel's breath, but Bree was already moving along the passageway. For days on end she and Dev had played hiding games in the forest. Would the places where she hid as a child still be there?

What if someone had built a house she didn't know about? What if angry men watched the paths?

When they reached the far end of the tunnel, Bree stopped at the ladder leading up to the trapdoor. "Mikkel, we have to pray. This might be your life, you know."

"I know, and I don't blame them. Why doesn't your father just turn me over to them?"

Bree wasn't willing to give up so easily. For a moment she stood there, her lips moving without sound. Finally she whispered just loud enough for Mikkel to hear. "Your hiding places, Lord."

"And protect Bree," Mikkel prayed.

But Bree felt more frightened than at any time in her life. The last time she tried to hide in these mountains she had known them well, but it hadn't been enough. When she escaped in the mountains of Norway, she had been ahead of those who searched for her. Now these were her own countrymen, her neighbors. Bree couldn't blame them for being angry. For years she had felt that same anger herself.

Then Bree remembered. Before now, she had often sensed God's direction. Like a small voice from deep inside she had felt His leading. Now His direction was clear. "Take the boat."

Instantly Bree knew what to do. If they took the river upstream, they could avoid the paths. But to get to the tall willow next to the river they would need to cross the most open pathway of all—the one that led through the gate up to the house. When they reached the willow would the boat she and Dev used to escape still be there?

For a moment longer, Bree stood there. *The boat?* she prayed silently. *I'm hearing You?*

In that moment Mikkel whispered into her ear. "Is there a boat somewhere nearby?"

Bree nodded. "Daddy says we'll come out in the meadow next to trees that will hide us until it's safe to move on."

Taking the candle, Mikkel went first. When he reached the trapdoor he found a latch that slid open with his first touch. As soon as he tested the door and found it also opened, he blew out the candle.

Lifting the door with his back, he crawled out, then held up the door for Bree. When she passed through, Mikkel made sure the turf fell back in place.

As Aidan had said, Bree and Mikkel were close to a cluster of trees. Together they waited there, listening, and heard only whispers of everyday sounds in the night air.

When they felt it safe to move on, they stayed inside the line of trees in the forest next to the meadow. At last they came to the river and the stepping-stones downstream from the path that led to the house. If they crossed on those stones, they would have to cross again to get back to the boat. But the far side of the river offered the shelter of trees.

Looking up at Mikkel, Bree whispered an explanation. He, too, felt they should cross the river. The moment they reached the other side, Bree felt better. The forest was totally dark—a darkness they needed. Bree found herself walking with outstretched arms to touch one tree trunk, then another, and pass beyond.

When Hammer stepped out from behind a tree, Bree jumped. "Take this," he whispered, offering his black cloak to Mikkel. "It will hide you better."

Quickly Mikkel put it on. "Go to the ship," he told Hammer. "Tell them to leave at once. I'm going to the monastery. Meet me in Dublin. If I'm not there in ten days, leave for home without me."

As Hammer started away, Mikkel whispered again. "Thanks, Hammer, for watching my back." When Hammer nodded, he tipped his head in respect.

At first the way was so dark that Bree could barely see where she was going. Then the moon came up, and its light filtered through the branches. When they drew close to the path leading to Bree's home, Mikkel touched her arm.

In that moment Bree heard it. Not far away, a stealthy sound.

Suddenly Mikkel pushed her aside, back against the trunk of a tree. Nearby, he disappeared into another shadow.

TWENTY-THREE

THE FOREVER GOOD-BYE

Moments later Bree heard the crunch of a cautious step on stony ground. As Bree held her breath, a shadow passed her not three feet away. A second shadow, then a third. Thick, strong bodies with only one clink— that of a sword.

In the silence that followed, Bree trembled. If she and Mikkel had passed through the gate, stayed on the path—

Bree didn't want to think about it. Instead, she had to trust that God would show them the rest of the way.

"Where's the boat?" Mikkel whispered from close behind her.

"Back across the river. Upstream. Under the willow."

When they reached the stepping-stones that led to

Bree's house, Mikkel took the lead. As though testing the night air to see what was there, he waited, looking around again. Without sound he and Bree crossed the stones and followed the river upstream. There they slipped under the long, trailing fronds of a willow and found the rowboat.

By now Bree had traveled enough to know how often fishermen in other parts of Ireland used a *curragh*—a boat covered with animal hides. Instead, her family used a long and narrow, low-sided boat that was easy to row in the Wicklow rivers. As soon as Bree climbed in, Mikkel pushed out from shore.

Upstream, she and Mikkel hid the boat and started dropping down the side of Brockagh Mountain. As they followed a long stone wall, Bree heard a branch snap. Instantly she dropped flat to the ground and tucked herself into the shadow of the wall. A few feet away, Mikkel did the same. Moments later a group of men passed by on the other side of the wall.

As Bree and Mikkel reached the valley of Glendasan, they crossed the river and followed another path over the side of Camaderry Mountain. In a forest of oak and Scotch pine, Mikkel suddenly whispered a warning.

Judging by the sound, it was an even larger group of men. This time Bree led Mikkel off the path into an undergrowth of holly, hazel, and other scrub.

When all was quiet again, Mikkel spoke softly. "Bree, leave me here. Go home! I'll find the way myself."

Bree refused. "We'll soon be there."

"It's not safe for you. If they find you're helping me——"

But Bree set out again, once more following the path that led them to the monastery. When they reached the gate in the high stone wall Bree hurried ahead. Out of long habit she pounded her special knock. Within moments the heavy door swung open.

Torch in hand, a monk stood before her. "Bree!" he exclaimed. "I thought it would be you. I heard you were back."

"And you remembered my knock. But please——"

As Mikkel stepped forward, the monk's eyes widened.

"We need help!" Bree said quickly. "The sanctuary stone——"

"Come in, come in——"

To Bree's surprise Mikkel walked straight over to the massive slab of rock inside the gate. Dropping on his knees before it, he reached up and placed both hands on the cross.

Bree barely heard the monk close the door and drop the strong wooden bar in place. She could only watch Mikkel. Then suddenly the quiet was broken.

As though a hundred men stood outside the gate, angry cries filled the night. Pounding shook the heavy wooden door. As terror leaped into Bree's heart, Mikkel leaped to his feet.

The moon was far above them now, shedding its light on the stones. From long practice Bree followed the path next to an inside wall. Then, as if he had heard the pounding on the gate, Brother Cronan hurried toward them.

"Come, child, come," he told Bree as if no years had passed between them. Moving without sound, he walked quickly ahead. As he brought Bree and Mikkel into a stone building, he turned back and barred the door.

When they entered a long hallway, Cronan again barred the door behind them. Then he spoke. "You're safe now, Mikkel. I've been expecting you."

Filled with surprise, Bree's words spilled out. "You know him?" she asked.

A torch set in the stone wall lit Cronan's face. "We are longtime friends," he said.

"Friends? Not enemies?"

"Friends." The monk's voice was sure and strong. "Mikkel has returned what he took for a time. He returned the Holy Book and the gems, and he wanted to pay interest on what he took. He has asked forgiveness. The Lord has forgiven him. I have forgiven him."

"So have I," Bree whispered, watching Mikkel. "So has my family."

Cronan smiled. "Good," he said simply.

When he spoke again it was to Mikkel. "When you finish talking, I'll be at the end of this hallway. I'll hide you well."

As Brother Cronan left them, his footsteps echoed on the stone walkway. When they sounded no more, Mikkel turned to Bree. In the light of the torch she saw shadows in his eyes. Then she saw the pain.

"I'm sorry, Bree," he said. "Keeping my promise took forever."

"Yes." The word caught in Bree's throat.

How can I help him for the years ahead? The years when we both remember what this time had been? But then Bree knew that she herself needed help.

Straight and strong, Mikkel stood before her, studying her face. "If I never see you again, I want you to know that I will never forget you."

"Nor I you."

"If we had met in a different time, a different place—"

"A different way—" Bree said. "But I'm not sorry, Mikkel. You have become a man of honor."

Suddenly she stopped, remembering Dublin. She still didn't know about Bjorn.

Bree swallowed hard, fighting the lump in her throat. When she spoke again, it was in faith for what she believed would happen. "You will be God's own man."

As though he could not tear himself away, Mikkel waited. When the silence stretched between them, Bree spoke gently.

"Thank you for the way you watched out for me. Thank you for the times you saved my life."

Mikkel's grin lit even his eyes. "It took a lot of doing, didn't it?"

Bree smiled. "A lot of doing."

"We covered great distances together."

Bree nodded. "You showed me the far places."

For a moment longer Mikkel waited, still studying her face as if he wanted to remember it always.

"Good-bye forever," Bree said softly.

"Not forever. I can't say forever."

For a moment Mikkel brushed his hands across his eyes. "When I am gone—when we don't see each other again, we must both remember God's forever promise. Hold it close to your heart."

Mikkel stopped, cleared his throat. When he spoke, his gaze met hers and his voice was strong. "The Lord Himself goes before you and will be with you."

"He will never leave you nor forsake you, Mikkel."

"Do not be afraid, Bree. Do not be discouraged."

Lifting her hand, Mikkel kissed her fingers. "Go with God," he said softly.

When she saw his eyes, she knew it was a forever good-bye. "Go with God," she whispered.

In the next moment he was gone.

TWENTY-FOUR

STRAIGHT AHEAD

In the days that followed, Tully did not come to the house. Often Bree walked to the place in the river where they had talked. Always she hoped that she would see him there. But one day followed the next and Tully never came.

On other mornings Bree climbed Brockagh Mountain and peered into the mists that hid the valley below. When a breeze came, she waited, looking off to the Irish Sea.

To Bree's surprise those waters no longer held the same fascination. No longer did she need to wonder what lay beyond them. She knew.

Instead of dreaming about far places, she started praying for her family and friends. At first her prayers centered on Tully. Then while at a neighbor's house she saw Tully talking with her sister Keely. When she saw the way Tully looked at her sister, Bree felt pain deep in her heart. But two nights later she remembered the way Keely looked at him.

Yes. There it was. Right in front of her, and at first Bree hadn't seen it. She hadn't understood, but Mam had. That was why she turned away instead of speaking her thoughts on Bree's first day home. Mam knew that Tully and her sister loved each other.

After five long years of thinking something would happen it was hard to understand why it didn't. *Why, God?* Bree asked. *Why?*

Quiet but sure, the message came with that inward sense Bree had learned to recognize. "I have called you to be a light to the nations."

At first the words upset her. She even felt angry. Then she drew a long, deep breath. "All right, Lord. I don't know where. I don't know how I can go. But I know You have called me, and I tell You yes."

That very day Bree walked to Tully's house. When he came to the door she asked if they could talk outside.

They walked to a bench overlooking the green hills of Ireland. The mists were soft on the land, the way Bree loved it best. There she gathered all the strength she had learned in the hard years of her captivity. "Tully, you waited for me to come home, didn't you?"

When he nodded, Bree went on. "You wanted to see me."

As though afraid to speak, Tully nodded again.

"Thank you," Bree said. "I don't know what I would have done if I had come home to find you wed. When times were hard, you were in my dreams. You were the thought that helped me remember there was a reason to come home."

"Bree—" Tully began, but she stopped him.

"It's not enough, Tully. You love Keely, don't you?"

Surprise flashed through his eyes, but when he spoke in the Irish, he used the heartwarming words Bree had always known. "Yes, I love Keely."

"And Keely loves you."

"You talked of it?"

"No." Bree smiled. "I saw it when she talked with you. Ask her to wed, Tully. It's what you both want, isn't it?"

Tully closed his eyes. When he took a long, deep breath, it was as if all the worries of the world had fallen from him. When he opened his eyes, his gaze was strong and clear.

Suddenly he laughed—the excited laugh of a boy let out of school. The joy-filled laugh of a young man who knew what he wanted and would go straight toward it.

"And you?" Tully asked, full of concern again. As they stood up and started walking, he caught Bree's hand and held it, as though to comfort her.

Startled, Bree wondered for a moment if she had misunderstood. But then she met his eyes. Both she and Tully knew it was his way of saying good-bye.

"Me?" Bree asked. "I don't know what will happen to me. But I'll walk straight ahead."

The knot was there in her stomach again. But from now on she would do everything she could to not let her sister or Tully know how she felt. How hard it was to say good-bye to yet another person.

Nor would she let anyone know her much deeper grief that Mikkel was gone forever. Only her brother Devin would guess. That is, if he wasn't too busy talking to Lil.

Determined to hide her loneliness, Bree searched her mind for the words she needed. When she knew them, she spoke from the depths of her heart.

"Tully, you will always be my special friend. And you and Dev will be good brothers."

TWENTY-FIVE

BJORN THE COBBLER

As soon as Brother Cronan believed it was safe, he gave Mikkel some trousers that looked distinctly Irish, a stout walking stick, and a heavy woven cloth that Mikkel wore over his head and shoulders when needed. Like a blanket, the cloth covered his sword and ended below his knees.

Cronan also gave Mikkel packages of food and a hand-copied New Testament wrapped in sealskin. A young monk who could walk or run as fast as Mikkel and knew the back ways to Dublin went with him.

Setting out in the dark of the night and a heavy rain, they were far from Wicklow by first light. Just the same, Mikkel felt relieved when he said good-bye to his new friend and passed through the gate into the Norse trading center. Inside the high walls there was protection that he desperately needed.

But he also wanted more—the opportunity to settle a long-overdue debt with Bjorn the cobbler. First Mikkel had wanted to be sure he could repay all he had stolen from the monastery. Now Mikkel still had enough from trading his goods to pay Bjorn.

When he reached the cobbler's shop, Mikkel stopped outside the open door. What if Bjorn threw him out before he could speak? What if the cobbler hated him so much that he heaped his anger upon him? Deeply wounded from saying good-bye to Bree, Mikkel didn't think he could handle any more.

Filled with dread, he forced himself to walk in. Though it had been five years since they met, Bjorn recognized him instantly.

"Mikkel! Good to see you again!"

"You really think so?" Mikkel stayed by the door in case he needed to run.

"I'm sure. How are you doing? How's your father?"

But Mikkel swept the questions aside. "I came to pay back what I stole from you."

Instantly Bjorn set down his hammer. As if afraid he would frighten Mikkel away, he stood up slowly. "I welcome you," he said. "I'm glad you're here."

When Mikkel did not answer, Bjorn said, "Sit down. Sit down."

Instead, Mikkel stayed on his feet.

From a hiding place inside his tunic he lifted out a bag with the cobbler's mark in the leather. "This is yours."

One by one, Mikkel took out four more, newer looking leather bags. "And this is yours. I want to pay back four times what I stole."

Bjorn stared at him. "Four times what you stole?"

"Like the tax collector who cheated people. You know, the little man who climbed up a tree? Devin told me about him."

Bjorn smiled. "Ah, yes. If your father knew, he would be proud of you for coming back."

"He doesn't know." Mikkel still needed to be honest. "When I brought home slaves from Ireland he said I'd never be free until I did what I could to set things right."

"Your father is a wise man. And now you are free?"

"I'm free, but I'm not happy yet." As though laughing at himself, Mikkel grinned.

"You know, I never met Bree," Bjorn said, watching Mikkel's face. "Where is she?"

"Home." Mikkel tried not to think about leaving her. Afraid that Bjorn would notice how he felt, Mikkel started to leave. But the cobbler spoke quickly.

"And Devin? What did he say about your bringing back the coins?"

"Devin?" Mikkel turned to him.

"Devin and Bree never talked to you about it?"

In that instant the pain went so deep in Mikkel's heart that he could barely speak. "They knew that I stole from my father's best friend in Dublin? All this time they knew and they never breathed a word?"

They were testing me, Mikkel thought. It made him angry. "Don't they trust me?"

"They probably wanted to let you take care of it yourself."

Mikkel sighed. All the wrong he had begun so long ago still stayed with him. All that he had done by returning the money to Bjorn seemed a waste. Bree and Devin knew he was guilty and would never know he had done his best to set things right.

Now Mikkel knew only one thing. He had to get away by himself. Away from Bjorn's eyes and all that he understood.

"Thanks, Bjorn," Mikkel said quickly. In that moment he could feel glad for only one thing—that he could meet the gaze of his father's friend. "Thanks for letting me come back."

As Mikkel left the cobbler's shop he walked quickly through the streets toward the wharf. At first all he could feel was relief. He had done his best to right his wrongs toward Brother Cronan and Bjorn. Now he hoped that his men had reached Dublin safely and that his ship lay waiting for him.

Home! Mikkel thought. Long ago he had sent word to his parents that he was in Greenland. But now many years lay between them. It warmed Mikkel's heart to remember the love of his father and mother. To remember that he had begun making friends with Cort—the brother he had ignored, but then started to know.

As though he was already sailing, Mikkel could feel the salt spray of the open sea. He would stand at the tiller, wait for the first sight of his native land. He would sail his ship through the fjords, watch the waterfalls tumble from the heights, and feel the welcome of his own village.

With every breath Mikkel took he wanted to be in Aurland again, among his friends and family. To sit around the table during the late-day meal and tell them about the world he had seen.

The sun was setting now, casting a golden light over the dark water of the River Liffey. But when he saw his ship at a distance, Mikkel turned away. It was too soon. He couldn't face his men. He couldn't look into the eyes of Garth, and Nola, and Hammer. He couldn't see their sympathy for how he felt.

Turning back, he again walked the streets of Dublin. Past one shop, one house after another he walked.

Though a Norse trading center, the roofs were thatched with straw and looked strangely Irish.

Finally, when the sky grew dark, Mikkel stopped. Looking up, he saw the stars reach down through a cloudless sky. In that moment he remembered another time, another night. From the edge of the sea, he and Bree and Devin had watched northern lights fill the sky. Streaks of white and green and red and purple. Reaching up high in the heavens. Reaching out over the water.

Bree. Suddenly it struck him. With all the pain of being ripped apart Mikkel felt it. *I will never see Bree again.*

Around him, the huts of the fishermen lay silent. The streets that would be filled with early morning shouts of "Fish for sale! Fish for sale!" were empty now. But Mikkel felt only the emptiness of his heart.

How could he live without her? How could anything ever seem good again?

Then the unfairness of it struck him. He had tried to set things right. He had asked God to lead and guide him. Was he to live the rest of his life alone?

On the night wind came the answer. "The Lord Himself goes before you and will be with you."

Suddenly the tears Mikkel wanted no one to see welled up in his eyes.

No more! he told himself. *No more tears!* All his life he had pushed them aside.

From the time he was very young he had been too big

to cry. But in the last two weeks he had wept as never before.

Deep inside, a sobbing began that shook every part of his being. Dropping down in the middle of the street, face to the ground, Mikkel finally whispered the words. "Good-bye, Bree. Good-bye forever."

He could never replace Bree in his heart. He would not even try. But then in the night still strangely quiet, under stars that shone in the darkness, he remembered what he decided that day on the rocky ridge. He couldn't change what he had already done. But he wanted the rest of his life to have some kind of purpose.

As the night wind stirred, peace settled over Mikkel. That's what he needed to go on. But moments later he felt uneasy from deep within. With it came a sense that he hadn't finished everything yet.

Mikkel groaned. All he wanted to do was to go home. To walk onto his ship, give the orders to sail, feel the tiller in his hand and the wind in his face.

I haven't finished everything yet?

Then Mikkel understood. As though he was still standing there, he saw himself in Bjorn's cobbler shop. He remembered his startling discovery. "Bree and Devin knew that I stole from you, my father's best friend in Dublin?"

"They never told you? They probably wanted to let you take care of it yourself."

They were testing me, Mikkel thought again. He felt glad he had done what was needed, but the sorrow of it struck him. Bree and Dev would never know.

For the first time Mikkel understood what he had seen when he turned quickly and Devin disappeared behind a house. *He wanted to know if I'd go to Bjorn the cobbler. Dev and Bree have forgiven me, but wanted to be sure that I set things right on my own.*

In that moment the certainty of what he must do filled Mikkel to overflowing. Rising up, he started running. Back to the river he ran. To his relief his *Conquest* still lay in the River Liffey, waiting for him.

When his guards saw Mikkel, they put out the walkway, and he hurried on board. Within moments he found Garth, and Nola, and Hammer. When Mikkel woke them, he saw the welcome in their eyes and the relief that he was safe. But then he explained.

"I have to go back. I can't leave without telling Bree and Dev that I returned the coins to Bjorn."

"No!" Garth cried out. "You must not go back."

"If you do, they'll kill you," Nola warned. "They're angry, Mikkel."

"If you return, you'll die for sure," Hammer said.

"If I don't go back, Bree and Dev will think I don't live what I believe."

"I'll tell them," Nola said.

"No, we will," Garth and Hammer said together.

Hammer leaned close into Mikkel's face. "I heard the men talk. They'll never let you escape a second time."

But Mikkel would not change his mind. "If I don't go back, Bree and Devin will never know that I set things right."

"Let me tell them," Nola offered again. "It will be safe for me."

Instead, Mikkel got ready to leave. "Stay here," he said when Garth wanted to sail once more to Arklow. "You'll be safe here, surrounded by Norsemen." Then to Nola—"I need some food for the journey."

When Mikkel opened his sea chest he found the cloak he like to wear with his red tunic. From the look of it Nola had cleaned the cloth and folded it carefully away. Mikkel took out his finest leggings and leather boots and pushed his best sword into the sheath at his waist. When his bundle of clothes was ready, he added the food Nola gave him. After wrapping it all in sealskin, he lifted it to his back. Then he walked over to the tiller of his ship. His *Conquest*.

For a time he stood there, just looking down at the tiller. Then he ran his hand along the wood and closed his fingers around the handle. Beneath the starlit sky he looked ahead and waited for the night wind to touch his face. When it did, he spoke once more.

"If I'm not back in six days set sail for home. When you reach Aurland, go to my father and mother. Remind my father of what he said—that I would never be really free until I did what I could to set things right. When they grieve because I am with them no more, tell them that now I am free."

When Mikkel stepped over the side of the ship and set foot once more on Irish soil, he heard only the sound of Nola's weeping.

Through the rest of the night Mikkel walked, his face set like flint toward the Wicklow Mountains. More than once he felt uneasy. More than once he turned suddenly and wondered if a shadow or two or three had slipped behind a tree. The thought filled him with terror.

With every part of his being Mikkel believed that he would not live through what lay ahead. What if something happened to him before he talked with Bree and Dev? They had to know. They *must* know that he had fulfilled every part of his promise to set things right.

Sometimes Mikkel walked. Sometimes he broke into a run. But now there was something he wondered. He had harmed so many people. If by some miracle he lived, could he possibly use his life for good? What could he do to make amends—to help people instead?

At dawn Mikkel reached the Sugar Loaf Mountains. From the surrounding meadows a large mountain rose suddenly to a high peak. Next to it stood a smaller mountain with three rounded slopes. The rising sun shone from behind, surrounding them with light.

As Mikkel walked toward the light, it filled his eyes, then his spirit. Again he heard a gentle whisper—Bree's words when they said farewell. "He will never leave you, nor forsake you."

When the day was full upon him Mikkel found trees away from the road and lay down behind a stone fence. All day he slept, exhausted by his trip to Dublin, his time with Bjorn, and now the walk back to the Wicklow Mountains.

As night fell, he set out again. Though he drew closer to danger, he walked tall with strength in his back and his head high. He would not go as a cowering slave, but as a son of the King of kings, knowing what he was asked to do.

Long before dawn, Mikkel reached the forest that grew close to the O'Toole farm. Before first light he swam in the river, welcoming the cool water that washed the dust of the road from him. Then he waited in the depths of the forest, ate, and slept.

Near sundown he opened his sealskin pack, took out his comb, and ran it through his hair and the beard trimmed close to his face. Quickly he put on his finest tunic and leather boots. When he fastened his dress cloak with the ring-pin Devin had made for him, Mikkel ran his fingers over the smooth surface. It was well-crafted, and Mikkel felt proud to wear it. More than that, it was a reminder that Devin was a good friend.

As terrible as it was to leave Bree, Mikkel knew he

would also miss Dev. Not since the brother closest to him died at sea had Mikkel shared that kind of friendship.

With his cloak flung over his shoulders and his best sword in its sheath he was ready to face the O'Tooles. But now he was not bringing Bree home. Instead, he felt compelled to explain—to let Bree and Devin know that he really had acted with honor.

As dusk gathered around him, Mikkel stole out quietly. At the stepping-stones across the river, he remembered Bree returning home. Again he felt a wave of grief. How soon would she marry Tully? He wanted only to tell her what he must and then leave at once, never to return again. Never to know the day that she wed.

No guards stood at the gate today. As Mikkel drew close he looked in every direction. In that moment he caught a movement out of the corner of his eye. Sword in his hand, he whirled around.

No shadow lingered under the trees. Whoever had been there was hidden. But the terror of being hunted down stayed with Mikkel. What if he never was able to tell Bree and Dev what they needed to know?

Then the words he had spoken to Bree sounded in his ears. "Do not be afraid. Do not be discouraged."

As Mikkel opened the gate, he remembered Brother Cronan's words. "Ask God to bring great blessing out of the wrong you have done."

Mikkel did.

TWENTY-SIX

PLEDGE OF HONOR

For the entire way up the path Mikkel fought his fear. More than once he turned quickly, trying to catch any person who might follow. Trying to understand where the danger lay.

Then he caught sight of the door—the bottom half closed, the top half still open to catch the sun and air. In that moment Brée looked out.

"Mikkel!" she exclaimed. Startled first and then glad. "You came back!"

Then fear entered her eyes. Coming outside, she glanced toward the meadow and the edge of the forest.

As though rooted to the ground, Mikkel stopped where he was. He hadn't been prepared for what it would mean to see her again. "Is Dev here? I must tell both of you something."

When Devin came to the door, the rest of the family followed him. With them was Brother Cronan.

"Son!" he exclaimed. "Don't you understand the danger?"

Mikkel spoke quickly. "There's something Bree and Dev need to know. When I went back to Dublin I returned the coins that I stole from my father's friend. I gave Bjorn the cobbler everything I took."

"Oh, Mikkel!" Tears of relief filled Bree's eyes, ran down her cheeks.

With one quick swipe Mikkel ran a hand across his own eyes. "I wanted you to know."

Standing there, stiff and straight, Mikkel had all he could do to not go to her. *She's Tully's true love*, he told himself. Turning, Mikkel started to leave.

But Devin hurried to him, clapped his back. "All this time—"

"You've been waiting to see what I would do."

Devin stepped back, nodded.

"You wanted to be sure that what I said I believe is real."

Again Devin nodded.

"Thank you," Mikkel said. Looking beyond Devin, he saw Bree watching. "Thank you for letting me do it on my own."

"Tell us more," Aidan said. "It was my friend Bjorn you went to see? He's also your father's friend?"

"My father's best friend in Ireland. They used to sail together. Then Bjorn married an Irish girl and settled down in Dublin."

"And now, it's all taken care of between you?"

Mikkel nodded.

"And, Cronan, everything is right between you and Mikkel?" Aidan spoke as though he knew the answer.

"He returned the gems and the book I sent on loan. I gave him a new one—one easier for the master of a ship to own."

Once more Mikkel turned, ready to leave, but not wanting to go. This time it was Bree's mother who stopped him. "We're just eating. Take food for your journey."

As the others started inside, Aidan summoned four of his men. "Watch the wall and gate and get additional men."

When Mikkel sat down at the table, he tried not to look at Bree. Tried not to guess her thoughts. When he heard the first warning, it came through the open window.

Alert to the danger, he turned his head. Yes, there it was. The voices of men gathering beyond the high earth embankment.

The uneasiness he had felt was not a mistake. This time he would not allow Bree to take him through the woods. Nor would he ask for sanctuary with Brother Cronan.

Then came the soft murmur of a voice quickly stilled. Aidan glanced toward the window, stood up, and walked to the door. For a moment he stood there. As he turned back into the room, he took out his sword and looked at Mikkel.

Concern filled Aidan's eyes. "Someone must have seen you on the way here."

"I will not run again," Mikkel said as he joined Bree's father by the door.

"I agree. You must not."

As Aidan stepped outside, Mikkel and the others followed him. In the twilight after the setting of the sun Mikkel saw the men gathered outside the gate. Some held torches. Others stood waiting. All had one look in their face. When they saw Mikkel they pushed forward, as if one person.

"Raider!" came the cry.

"Destroyer of all that we love!"

Mikkel closed his eyes, them opened them again. Dimly he felt Bree and Devin, then the rest of their family move up. Bree's mother, Keely, Cara, Jen, even Adam. With them stood Brother Cronan.

From the midst of the crowd a man pushed three people toward the gate. Garth, Nola, and Hammer!

"No!" Mikkel cried out. "I told you to stay in Dublin, to let me come alone!"

"We could not!" Garth said. Like Hammer, his hands

were tied behind his back. Nola stood between them.

When loud voices blurred the sound of Garth's words, Mikkel looked around. Only four men guarding the gate? It would be no problem for a crowd of this size to overwhelm them. But then Mikkel saw additional men stationed at different places around the inside of the ring fort.

As the crowd kept growing, Mikkel felt their anger build. Then Mikkel felt more. He could not bear to have Bree and her family see his blood spilled on their doorstep.

"Stop!" he called out, but no one obeyed. Instead, they kept pushing forward until the people at the gate were jammed tightly against it. Sure that they would soon try to break through, Mikkel pulled his sword from its sheath, walked toward them, and waited. Immediately the crowd hushed.

In the silence Aidan's voice rang out. "Who offers their challenge to fight Mikkel?"

"I do!" a man at the front of the crowd lifted his sword.

"Who will be his witness—his backup?"

Another man called out.

"Who will be Mikkel's witness—his backup?"

"I will!" called Hammer.

"You who are Irish know that five days must pass between the challenge and the fight," Aidan said. "What have you to say for yourself?"

"I will wait," answered the man who offered the challenge. "Mikkel took my sister away."

"Mikkel?" Aidan asked.

In that moment Mikkel knew what to do. Standing his tallest, he called out in a voice that all could hear. "If you wish, I will wait," he said. "But I can offer you something better. I call upon you, good men of Wicklow, to hear this.

"I have wronged you. First, I ask your forgiveness for what I have done."

At once the murmur of angry voices swelled. But Aidan motioned for them to be quiet. "All of us agree that Mikkel wronged us. But he has asked forgiveness, and forgiveness can give us peace. I have forgiven him. My wife, Maureen, has forgiven him. Bree and Devin have forgiven him."

Outside the gate, Nola stepped forward. "And I have forgiven Mikkel."

Heads turned. Though Nola came from farther away, she had lived in the Wicklow Mountains.

From the back of the crowd a tall man started toward the gate. The crowd opened before him. "I, Bjorn the cobbler, have forgiven him. Though he wronged me, Mikkel set it right. He paid back four times what he owed."

When Bjorn finished speaking, the murmur of voices rose again. Mikkel glanced from one Irishman to the next.

How many of these men knew and respected Bjorn from his honest trade in Dublin?

Then Brother Cronan stepped forward and every voice fell silent. "I, too, have forgiven Mikkel. In the eyes of God he is forgiven. He has returned the stolen gems. He has returned the Holy Book I used to bargain for your lives. And he has offered a gift because he is sorry for what he did."

Cronan looked from one end of the crowd to the other. "Your honorable and much-loved chieftain is right. Forgiveness can give us peace."

In silence the leader at the front of the crowd bowed his head in respect, first to Brother Cronan, then to Aidan. But when he turned to Mikkel, the anger was still in the man's face.

In that moment Mikkel held up his sword and waited as the crowd hushed.

Again Mikkel spoke in a voice all could hear. "I lay down my sword not in disgrace, because I have refused to fight, but in honor, because I offer you something better. I ask that you give me the opportunity to make amends."

Mikkel paused, moved closer to the crowd, and laid his sword on the ground between them. "Good men of Wicklow, I cannot change what happened with the Vikings who came here before me. But I want to do what I can to make amends for my raid. If you tell Brother Cronan the names of the people you lost five years ago, I will try to find them. If they wish to come back, I will do my best to free them."

Devin and Adam brought a table and bench from the house and set them down just inside the gate. Then Aidan gave Brother Cronan a newly scraped goat skin and quill pen. But when he sat down at the table, the men stood without moving.

From one to another Mikkel looked, studying their faces. Without doubt each of these men had a sister or brother, a father or mother, uncle or aunt taken in his raid. Yet how could they possibly trust him to care for that loved one?

Silently Mikkel prayed. Then he knew what to do.

Picking up his sword, Mikkel held it out to Bree's father, the much-loved chieftain of the men who stood before him. Bowing low, then meeting Aidan's gaze, Mikkel spoke.

"I give you this sword as my pledge of honor that I will never again willfully harm a member of your family, nor the people you lead so wisely."

His gaze never leaving Mikkel's face, Aidan spoke. "I receive this, your sword, as your pledge of honor. You will never again willfully harm a member of my family, nor the people I lead. In addition, you will do all that is in your power to restore the people taken away from their families."

Aidan turned to the crowd. "Because Mikkel has

given you a legal way to dissolve this dispute, it is illegal for you to hold him to your challenge of combat."

Standing back, Mikkel waited. Aidan opened the gate. With slow but sure steps the leader of the group started forward. "My mother," he said, and Brother Cronan wrote down her name.

"My brother," said another. Then two sisters. A mother, a son, and more.

With each name Mikkel flinched inside. *What have I done? How can I ever keep this new promise?*

Then, as the crowd thinned, Mikkel saw Tully standing inside the earthen wall. More than ever before, Mikkel understood why Bree had mistaken him for Tully.

With windblown blond hair much like Mikkel's, the tall young man stood straight and lean, and strong. Just seeing him, the pain rose again within Mikkel. Then across the clearing Tully smiled at Bree. As Bree smiled back, Mikkel felt as if his heart were torn in two.

When the line of people dwindled, Mikkel stopped at the table where Brother Cronan took the names. As the last person stood before him, the monk wrote the name, waited for the ink to dry, and rolled up the parchment.

"God go with you," he said, as he gave it to Mikkel.

Unable to answer, Mikkel nodded. Again he started to leave. But this time Bree's father stopped him. "You are a man of honor," Aidan said. "You are welcome any time you wish to visit my home."

Before Bree's mother, Mikkel bowed low. Then he stopped in front of Bree.

"I can't say good-bye again," he told her. "Happy birthday for tomorrow."

Bree blinked, seeming surprised that he remembered. In the light of the torches she looked up into his face. When she met his gaze a tear welled up, spilled over, and ran down her cheek. As more tears followed, she tried to speak, but could not. And still Mikkel stood before her.

Then he knew. She, too, had nothing more she could say.

As the moment stretched long between them, Mikkel tipped his head in a farewell nod. Turning, he walked swiftly away. With his long stride he started down the pathway to the gate. Bjorn and Hammer, Garth, and Nola fell in behind him.

To Mikkel's relief he saw that only two people remained. But then he saw it was Devin on one side of the path and Tully on the other. Without looking toward Tully, Mikkel spoke to Devin. "You have taught me well, my friend."

Before Devin could answer, Mikkel walked on, but Tully called after him.

"A word with you, Mikkel!"

When Mikkel pretended he hadn't heard, Tully spoke louder. "A word, Mikkel."

Knowing he had no choice, Mikkel stopped. If he

didn't, Tully would call loud enough for the men who had scattered to come back. Suddenly all the frustration and grief Mikkel had felt since coming back to Ireland boiled up, ready to spill over.

But Tully stepped forward. "You aren't leaving without talking to Bree, are you?"

Mikkel straightened. Of all he had suffered, this was the worst. "I'm not going to stay around to watch you get married, if that's what you mean."

TWENTY SEVEN

THE FAR PLACES

On the morning of Bree's eighteenth birthday, she opened her eyes and wished she didn't have to celebrate. Exactly five years had passed since the day Mikkel's ship took her away.

What good could there be in a day such as this? Her dreams once again lost, given over to something better for her sister and Tully. In spite of knowing that would be best for both of them, the sharp edge of Bree's disappointment was still there. She had held a dream about Tully for too long. Would she ever know what it meant to not hurt inside?

Lying in the darkness before dawn, Bree thought about it. But something else kept crowding in. Her first sight of Mikkel on the ship that took her away from all she loved. Mikkel again, on the coast of northern Ireland where he set Devin free. The long voyage where she had been seasick for days. How Mikkel took her to the tiller and commanded her to look at the horizon.

Then the mountains near the sea where she and Lil escaped and managed to hide. The Aurland Fjord. The voyages to the Norwegian king, to Iceland, and Greenland. Then that day of all days when she, Dev, and Mikkel followed Leif Erikson into a new world.

Sometimes Bree thought that's what hurt most of all. That in their journeys they had experienced such a big world, yet hadn't been able to keep the best of it. But then Bree knew it was more.

Was it the fighting with Mikkel that she missed? Though it didn't happen as often as she wanted, she liked getting the best of him.

Trying to push aside her thoughts, Bree got up and dressed quickly. As silently as on the morning of her thirteenth birthday, she slipped out the door.

In the gray light before dawn she passed through the forest and saw that the blueberries were ready. Catching up a handful, she ate as she went. But as she walked she remembered.

Blueberries. Leif's Camp. With everything Bree did, there was a memory attached. A memory of far places, but also a memory of people she had known.

On that day filled with blueberries, Hammer had found bog ore. While building the smithy he asked, "Don't you hate Mikkel?" and Bree shook her head. "Not anymore."

It started her wondering. *When did it change?*

For months she had hated Mikkel. Yet her feelings toward him had changed from hatred to distrust. Then to her surprise she learned to respect him. To even like him as a friend. At last she began to understand that he could be God's chosen man—a leader who would take the hard times he had known and lead others. But it hadn't been enough.

Too much hurt lay between them. When the change came in Mikkel she still questioned. She needed to guard her heart.

For too long she had thought of Mikkel as someone who wanted only wealth and fame. Even at the monastery she still faced the question. Mikkel had done his best to make peace with Brother Cronan. But would Mikkel return the stolen coins to Bjorn and set things right?

Only in the moment when he said good-bye did Bree believe that she knew the answer. In faith she told him, "You have become a man of honor. You will be God's own man."

From that time on she had believed in his commitment to live with honor. She had felt certain that she could trust him. But she needed to see him live it out, and he had.

Deep in her heart Bree felt the excitement of seeing that happen. But it was too late. She would never see him again.

When Bree reached her favorite place on Brockagh Mountain, the mists of Ireland filled the valleys and hid her view of the sea. On every birthday except when she was gone, she had watched the sun rise above the sea. Now she sat down on a large rock and waited for a breeze to blow the mists away. Waited for the sun to appear above the horizon. Waited to begin her birthday and her new year.

Strange, Bree thought, as she often did. From an early age she had wanted to know what lay beyond the Irish Sea. She had never expected how hard it would be to learn. But now that she was home again she wondered, "What next?"

As the mist held, Bree waited. Then the fog thinned just enough to see a small part of the valley below. In that moment the thought came.

Home is where the heart is.

It startled Bree. Yes! At the strangest time her father told her that. He had seen her and Mikkel together. He understood. He wanted to help her in the moment when she wondered what to do.

But she had missed it. Even last night when she saw the person Mikkel had become, she had not been able to utter a word. As he started to leave again, she ran into the house, unable to watch.

Mikkel had risked his life to tell them he was honest. He wanted them to know that he was living what he believed. Now he was gone. Gone forever. And her heart went with him.

Leaning forward, Bree buried her head in her lap. What good would it do to begin her new year without Mikkel? What did it matter that this was a new day and that she was home again?

As the tears came, Bree could not stop them. Long sobbing gasps spilled from her. No longer could she hold back the pain and loneliness of watching Mikkel leave.

When at last she could speak, she cried out to the mountains. "Oh, God, Mikkel is gone! Gone forever!"

Only then did she hear a sound behind her. "No, I'm not," Mikkel said. "I'm still here."

Bree whirled around. "You're here?"

"I wanted to wish you happy eighteenth birthday."

Bree tried to smile. The birthday she had dreaded, thinking she would be too old to wed.

As Mikkel sat down next to her he went on. "I wanted to give you the best birthday gift I could. Last night as I was leaving, Tully stopped me. He asked, 'You aren't leaving without talking to Bree, are you?' And he told me the Irish way. If a man wishes to wed his true love, he must talk to her father."

"You talked to Daddy?" Bree couldn't believe it. "What did he say?"

"He asked me questions for three or four hours. We talked long into the night. Then he woke your mother, and we talked more. 'Will you be a caring lad?' she asked. 'One who understands the heartbeats of his wife?' 'And will you walk in the ways of God?' your father asked."

"All that was going on, and I slept right through it?" Bree asked. Then she remembered. She had cried herself to sleep. No wonder she didn't hear the murmur of their voices.

Mikkel's eyes were wet. "Bree, I want to be a caring lad, a man who understands your heartbeats. But most of all, I want to be a man after God's own heart—a man who listens, and obeys, and serves Him."

As Bree looked into Mikkel's eyes, she felt the stillness. Then she understood what God had done. He wasn't too soon, or too late.

"There will be Irish who never trust you," Bree said.

"I know."

"War will come," she warned. "War led by strong leaders who want to cast the Norsemen completely out of Ireland."

"I know."

"But how?" Bree asked. "How can we live here? How can we live in Norway? You have your family. I have mine."

When Mikkel laid his hand across hers, the steadiness in his eyes caught Bree's breath. "We can never forget our families. We can never leave them out of our hearts. They are life to us, and we are life to them. But I will make my living as a merchant. Because I know the sea, we will use it to place stepping-stones between our families."

"Stepping-stones?" Across the vast seas they had traveled? The North Sea was too filled with storms. The North Atlantic too large, too deep, too cold for stepping-stones. Though smaller, the Irish Sea, the Norwegian Sea, were still too big for stepping-stones. Stepping-stones could only be used for boggy ground or shallow places in a river.

And then Bree caught it. Something Mikkel understood.

"The water," she said. "Your ship, the *Conquest*. It will be God's way of bringing us wherever He wants us to go."

The mists of Ireland still surrounded them. As Bree looked into Mikkel's face she gently lifted the windblown hair that hung down over his forehead. The bruise that started it all no longer showed. But Bree still saw Mikkel crossing the stepping-stones, saw him falling into the river.

"Your parents, Mikkel? How will your parents feel about you marrying a slave?"

Mikkel's grin spread into his eyes. "My parents love you. They've always been on your side."

Suddenly he laughed. "They know better than anyone that you do not make a good slave."

Then he laughed again. "Do you know what your father told me last night? In much of the world a bride brings money or property to her husband when they marry. Is Ireland the only place on earth where a groom gives money or property to the father of the bride?"

Bree smiled, putting on her most dignified, daughter-of-a-chieftain look.

"A man pays for the privilege of marrying *you?*" Mikkel asked.

When Bree laughed with him, it sounded like a bell, its clear notes ringing across the valley. "I always knew that the Irish honor their women," she said.

As though he heard the music in her laughter, Mikkel put his hand over hers. Slipping his arm around her shoulders, he waited with her.

Together they felt the breeze and watched it chase the fog away. Together they stood to face the Irish Sea and greet the dawn. In the clear air that came like a special gift, they gazed across the water.

In the moment when the first red edge of the sun shone above the horizon, Mikkel turned to her. "Happy birthday, Bree," he whispered. "Happy new year and new life."

As Bree looked from the sun into his eyes, the depth of her love welled up within her. *Tried*, she thought. *Tested.* And best of all, *approved by God.*

"I love you, Bree," Mikkel said, his voice stronger now.

"I love you, Mikkel." The words felt strange on Bree's lips, but then after a moment, they didn't. How often in these days since returning home had she thought them to herself? And now her home would take in the world. Her home would be wherever she and Mikkel were.

Reaching out, he touched the side of her face. "I love you, Briana," he said again. "Will you marry me?"

With the sunlight full upon them and her gaze meeting Mikkel's, Bree gave her answer. "Yes, yes, yes!"

Then Mikkel glanced beyond her. "Look!" he said softly.

As the sun rose over the water, they could see the far places—the distant blue mountains across the Irish Sea.

"It's Wales," Bree told him.

"I've never been there," Mikkel answered. "Would you like to go?"

Bree smiled. "At the right time," she said.

DISCUSSION QUESTIONS

If you use Viking Quest novels for your family read-aloud times, school, or homeschooling, you'll find additional resources and discussion questions for earlier novels in this series on my website: www.loiswalfridjohnson.com.

1. Courage? What is it? For five novels we've talked about the courage to win. We've seen courage in the lives of Bree, Devin, and Mikkel in many different ways. But how can you and I have courage in our own lives? Does having courage mean that you are never afraid? If not, what *does* it mean to have courage?

2. Who was your favorite character in this novel? For what reasons? How did you feel about what happened to that character? Why do you feel that way?

3. What did you think was the most exciting part of the novel? Why?

4. How did the houses that Leif built help him deal with the climate he knew in Greenland? What did Leif and his expedition use for cooking? warmth? protection? Can you think of a modern-day style of house that reminds you of the houses that Leif built? (If you live in a cold climate it will be easier for you to answer.) How is that house similar to Leif's? How is it different?

5. When Leif stepped into the small boat to go ashore at the place that became his base, Bree realized the importance of what she was seeing. What do you think would be the most exciting part about being the first person to step foot in a new land? What might be the dangers and hardships of being the first person or group in a new land?

6. Have you had circumstances in your life where at first you didn't understand the importance of what was happening? (An example might be moving to a new

home or location.) How did such a time affect the rest of your life?

7. When the *Greenlanders' Saga* says that Leif named a place Helluland or Markland, it means that with the naming, he claimed these lands for himself and his family. Have you ever had the opportunity to name a new place? Where? How did you choose the name? If you haven't named something, think about a place that interests you and decide what you would like to call it.

8. When characters talked about the L'Anse aux Meadows location being a gateway, what did they mean? Find that gateway on your map. Where does it lead? Give your reasons why this location could be important to Leif.

9. Make a list of words that are unfamiliar to you. Look up their meaning. How can you use these new words in your writing or conversation? How does the place where you live affect the words that you know or don't know?

10. When Mikkel told Bree he would do what he promised, what did you think he would *really* do? Why did you feel that way?

11. When Bree talked with Mikkel about how she had rescued him from drowning, what was the cause and effect that he saw in his own actions? What did he decide to do about it?

12. What are some possible reasons why people in earlier times married younger than they often do now?

13. Why was it important for Bree to wait and see whether Mikkel would live what he said he believed?

14. What did you think about Vikings before you started reading this series? How have your ideas changed?

15. Now let's talk about courage again. How did Mikkel feel about trying to set right what he had done? What made him most afraid? What kind of help did he get? Would you call him courageous? Why or why not?

FOR FURTHER STUDY:

A. If you'd like to find the markers given in the first chapter of this novel, use a detailed Newfoundland/ Labrador map. Imagine yourself standing on Belle Isle, a high, rocky island described by Helge Ingstad as a fairy-tale castle rising from the sea. Give Belle Isle the name of Current Island, then look south toward what is now called the Strait of Belle Isle (Straumfjord or Current Fjord). The distinctive markers named are presently called Cape Bauld (the round head of a cape) and Cape Onion (to the right), which form the entrance to the L'Anse aux Meadows area. Then Great Sacred Island (with high vertical rock rising from its shore), Beak Point, and the headland called the rocky ridge in this story. The building site known in the novel as Leif's Camp is now called L'Anse aux Meadows National Historic Site and is located on Epaves Bay.

B. In the story Bree looks for a baby seal, known by later settlers as a "whitecoat." When I asked David Morrow, Park Interpreter, Gros Morne National Park of Canada, how a mother seal would react to Bree's curiosity, he said, "The mother harp seal might let a person quite close to the pup, depending on the circumstances. If the adult female has a lead of open water nearby, she will desert the pup and escape to the water." In Viking times the usual predators on ice floes were polar bears. How could that affect a mother seal's behavior? Using reference sources, what else can you learn about the behavior and habits of seals? How far do some of them travel? What international agreements and laws protect seals now?

C. What can you find out about the eastern New Brunswick area that would make that location for Hóp a
strong possibility? (Try an encyclopedia such as *World
Book,* the Internet, or travel guidebooks from your
local library.)

If you or your family would like to visit the L'Anse
aux Meadows Viking site in Newfoundland, see the
acknowledgment section for the contacts you need.

*Thank you for the heartwarming response you have shown
toward the Viking Quest series. Thank you for your letters, e-mails,
and enthusiasm. I'm sorry that with this novel we need to say
good-bye to this series. I also like Bree, Devin, Mikkel, and their
families and friends. I hope you'll keep thinking about them for a
long time.*

*Courage is catching. May you receive the gift of contagious
courage from those around you. Even more important, may you
live in such a way that you inspire courage in others.*

*As always, every book I write is a special letter from me to
you!*

Love and blessings—
Lois

ACKNOWLEDGMENTS

Soon after local fisherman George Decker led explorer Helge Ingstad to some slightly elevated, very overgrown mounds in Newfoundland, our history books needed to be rewritten. For years Helge had searched for the place described in the Vinland sagas—a Viking settlement in North America. When he saw the Newfoundland site in 1960, Helge said to himself, "This is it!"

Dr. Ingstad was particularly struck by the similarities of the site to that of Erik the Red's home in Greenland. However, many questions needed to be answered. Was this a site used by North American Aboriginal Peoples, whalers, or fishermen? To be certain that there was a

Norse presence in this location there needed to be archaeological excavations.

From 1961 to 1968 archaeologist Dr. Anne Stine Ingstad led the work in which eight building sites and other features were excavated. Scholars from Canada, Iceland, Sweden, the United States, and Norway participated. Their work proved that the ruins were the remains of buildings occupied in the early 11th century by Vikings. A detailed description of the Ingstad findings is found in *The Viking Discovery of America,* by Helge Ingstad and Anne Stine Ingstad.

The people in Leif Erikson's expedition were the first Europeans known to have established a site in North America. Today that site is called L'Anse aux Meadows and is located at the top of the Great Northern Peninsula in western Newfoundland. The only authenticated Viking settlement in North America, L'Anse aux Meadows has been designated a national historic site by the Historic Sites and Monuments Board of Canada and in 1978 became a UNESCO World Heritage Site primarily due to what it tells us about the worldwide movement of peoples.

Though other long-ago sources mentioned the discovery of a new world, people have especially focused on the events described in the Vinland Sagas. The *Greenlanders' Saga* and *Erik the Red's Saga* were not written by eyewitnesses but passed orally from one person to the next.

In the early thirteenth century they were written down independently in Iceland.

These sagas contain stories about exceptional events such as voyages that occurred more than two hundred years before. They also gave important landmarks and information needed by a seafaring people. Helge Ingstad's discovery brought these sagas that began as oral history into the realm of "Yes, it actually happened."

From 1973–76 excavation continued under Parks Canada. I am deeply indebted to Dr. Birgitta Linderoth Wallace, Senior Archaeologist (emeritus), Atlantic Service Centre, Parks Canada, for helping me see the Vinland sagas in a new way. I first became acquainted with Birgitta's work through her chapters in the Smithsonian publication, *Vikings: The North Atlantic Saga.*

Birgitta tells how Ólafur Halldórsson convincingly demonstrated that the two sagas had different purposes. While the *Greenlanders' Saga* was written to provide an historical record of the Vinland exploration, *Erik the Red's Saga* was intended to enhance the role of Gudrid and Thorfinn Karlsefini and help their descendants.

As I used this understanding to guide my thinking, I found that Birgitta's wisdom helped me reconcile and deal with the differences between the two sagas. In addition to her in-depth knowledge about archaeological findings, Birgitta gave me fresh insights about the cultural aspects of the wider Norse world. I also value Birgitta's translation of the description of Leif given in *Erik's Saga*, for it is as close to the original Old Norse wording as possible. I've adapted that translation into Mikkel's farewell to Leif.

L'Anse aux Meadows is also thought to be the first place in North America where ore was smelted to produce iron. The equipment was identical to that used in Iceland and Norway.

Because of its location on the Strait of Belle Isle, it is believed that L'Anse aux Meadows served as a base for exploration in the Gulf of St. Lawrence and an overwintering place where ship repair took place. The buildings could house seventy to ninety people and had large storerooms. At this historic site three of the buildings and the smithy have been replicated. Each summer Parks Canada interpreters, wearing period Viking dress, reenact what life may have been like at the Viking camp. Their activities are based on the archaeological evidence uncovered there. For more information see www.pc.gc.ca/lanseauxmeadows or call L'Anse aux Meadows at (709) 623-2608 or (709) 458-2417 off season.

Norstead, a Viking Port of Trade, is nearby. Norstead houses *Snorri*, a full-scale replica of a Viking ship, and offers programs for families and schoolchildren. See www.vikingtrail.org or www.norstead.com. Phone 709-454-8888 for more information.

See www.parkscanada.gc.ca for information about

national parks, historic sites, and numerous places of interest in Newfoundland and Labrador.

For more than 150 years people have debated about the location and existence of Vinland. Excavations at L'Anse aux Meadows revealed butternuts, which have never grown in that area. The place closest to Newfoundland in which butternuts grow is in the St. Lawrence River valley, just east of Quebec City in north-eastern New Brunswick, a bit inland from the Bay of Chaleur, the Miramichi, and other river estuaries. Wild grapes also grow in the same area. Prior to the seventeenth century, ancestors of the Micmacs had canoes built with oil-soaked moose skins over a wood frame.

The Gudrid introduced in this novel is remembered as a world traveler. Soon after Leif rescued the shipwrecked people, many of them became ill, possibly because of the cold and exposure they experienced on the skerry. That winter Leif's father, Erik the Red, and Gudrid's husband died. In time Gudrid married Leif's brother, Thorstein, and when he died, Gudrid married Thorfinn Karlsefni, an Icelandic merchant. Their son, Snorri, is the first child born of European parents in North America. In addition to traveling to Norway, Iceland, Greenland, and Vinland, Gudrid also traveled to Rome.

After his father's death, Leif took over Erik's role as supreme chieftain of the Greenland settlements. It appears that because of his additional responsibilities Leif was not able to return to what we now call the New World. Yet Leif's place in history as organizer and leader of the first expedition is confirmed in a variety of important ways and especially through the archaeological findings in Newfoundland. Because of his foresight, wise planning, care for those under his leadership, and cautious yet go-ahead-and-do-things spirit, we see in Leif a courage that can inspire us all.

The fourth Viking Quest novel, *Heart of Courage*, describes the events that took place in Iceland and Greenland during the year 1000. When Leif returned from Norway with the message of Christianity, his mother, Thjodhild, said, "Yes!" and requested baptism. She is the first recorded convert to the new faith in Greenland. Subsequently she built a small church in a fold of the land away from the house.

After years of wondering where this building was located and whether the saga spoke truth, archaeologists verified the location of Thjodhild's church. Recently an ecumenical group from many nations built a small chapel modeled after that church. There is reasonable certainty that the first recorded baptism in Greenland took place in this area.

Though Vikings came as raiders, they encountered Christianity and some became Christians. King Olaf Tryggvason was one of them.

In 1014, only a short time after Mikkel faced the justifiably angry men of the Wicklow Mountains, High King Brian Boru defeated a joint army of Vikings and the King of Leinster at Clontarf, but was himself killed. The influence of men from the North continues to be revealed through archaeological findings and our knowledge of relationships that developed through the years.

The Glendalough Monastery in County Wicklow, a short distance south of Dublin, remains an exceptionally beautiful and meaningful place to visit. Address: Glendalough Visitor Centre; telephone +353-404 45325/45352.

In addition to my gratitude for the help of Dr. Birgitta Wallace, I offer my heartfelt thanks to each of the following people. If I have made an error or misinterpreted the information they gave me, the responsibility is mine.

In Newfoundland:

Loretta Decker, Historic Site Supervisor, L'Anse aux Meadows National Historic Site of Canada. Loretta is also the granddaughter of George Decker, who led Helge Ingstad to the site. Thanks, Loretta, for your thoughtful answers to countless questions about the long-ago, as well as the present, and for putting me in contact with additional resources.

Lloyd Decker, the son of George Decker, worked with the Ingstads from 1960 and turned the first sod for their dig. Lloyd also worked with the provincial and federal governments and for nine years was the only guide at L'Anse aux Meadows. He retired as the maintenance supervisor.

Madge Decker, who along with her husband, Lloyd, helped me discover and appreciate the natural beauty of the area.

Mark Pilgrim, Historic Site Interpreter, who is trained in Viking-age blacksmithing and produces items for the site.

David Morrow, Park Interpreter, Gros Morne National Park of Canada, for help with wildlife details and the ice scenes. Also a UNESCO World Heritage site, Gros Morne has been called Newfoundland's scenic masterpiece, www.parkscanada.gc.ca/grosmorne.

In Norway:

Anders Ohnstad, historian, author, and teacher; Ingvar Vikesland, able communicator, teacher, and headmaster, now principal, Local History Center in Aurland.

Anders not only helped me think through some of the concepts that shaped the series, he and Ingvar have now provided details and read portions of five manuscripts. *Tusen takk!*

In Northern Ireland:

Elaine Roub, faithful encourager and provider of details.

In the Republic of Ireland:

Glendalough Visitors Centre, Glendalough Monastery, County Wicklow, for their historical information and tours.

Christopher Stacey, Mountain Leader, Footfalls Walking Holidays, County Wicklow, for a great hike, providing insights and details, and offering encouragement, www.walkinghikingireland.com.

In the United States:

Michael and Lizabeth Towers for helping my characters sail and for reading portions of the manuscript; Sarah Chaffee for a key thought about the theme of this novel; Karin Johnson and her mother-daughter reading group for asking great questions.

Thanks for a variety of reasons to Ken Gire, Chuck and Dee Brown, Giles Ekola, Sue Davidson, Bob and Ronda Elmer, Vernon Hedge, Randy Klawitter, Jim Smith, Chuck Peterson, Park Hunter, Judy Eng, Darrel Gadbois, Judy Werness, the Douglas County Library, my Thursday morning group, and my longtime friends and encouragers.

My agent, Lee Hough, and Alive Communications; Barbara LeVan Fisher for her cover design and logo; Greg Call for his cover illustration and inside art.

The great folks at Moody: Dave DeWit; Andy McGuire; Pam Pugh; Amy Peterson; Lori Wenzinger; Carolyn McDaniel; John Hinkley; Gene Eble; Cessandra Dillon, and the entire team.

Once again my husband, Roy, has been my faithful, around-the-clock encourager. More than that, God has used him to help me see courage lived out in daily life. Thanks, Roy, for the way your Norwegian heritage has enriched our marriage. Thanks for the fun and the privilege of being your wife.

My gratitude to each person who translated the Vinland Sagas and spent years of study to ferret out their secrets. I offer my fictional interpretation of what happened with humility and within the framework of my ever-present need to meet a deadline. I have found the following books, magazines, and websites especially helpful:

Carlsson, Dan, and Owen, Olwyn, editors, *Follow the Vikings*, Council of Europe Cultural Routes guidebook describing fifty sites that are highlights in the Viking world, Viking Heritage, 1996, www.hgo.se/viking. Dan Carlsson is also the publisher and editor-in-chief of Viking Heritage Magazine, Gotlund University, Visby, Sweden.

Cook, Ramsay, introduction, *The Voyages of Jacques Cartier*, University of Toronto Press, Toronto, © 1993.

Delaney, Mary Murray, *Of Irish Ways*, Harper and Row Publishers, New York, © 1973.

Fitzhugh, William W. and Ward, Elisabeth I., editors, *Vikings: The North Atlantic Saga*, Smithsonian Institution Press, Washington and London, in association with the National Museum of Natural History, © 2000 by the Smithsonian Institution.

Haywood, John, *Encyclopaedia of the Viking Age*, Thames and Hudson, Inc., New York, NY, © 2000.

Ingstad, Helge and Ingstad, Anne Stine, *The Viking Discovery of America*, Checkmark Books, New York, © 2001.

Joyce, P. W., *A Social History of Ancient Ireland*, vol. 1 & 2, originally published 1903, republished in the U.S., Kansas City, MO: Irish Genealogical Foundation, © 1997.

Rodgers, Michael and Losack, Marcus, *Glendalough: A Celtic Pilgrimage*, The Columba Press, Dublin, © 1996.

Russell, Franklin, *The Illustrated Natural History of Canada: The Atlantic Coast*, N.L.S. Natural Science of Canada Limited, Toronto, © 1970.

Sturluson, Snorri, *From the Sagas of the Norse Kings*, Dreyers Forlag, Oslo, © 1967.

Thorsson, Örnólfur, editor, *The Sagas of Icelanders*, Viking, Penguin Group, New York, Leifur Eiriksson Publishing Ltd., © 1997, first published by Viking Penguin, 2000.

Viking magazine, Anna Befort, Editor, Sons of Norway, Minneapolis, MN, www.sonsofnorway.com.

The Viking Network website, sponsored by The Nordic Council of Ministers, www.viking.no. This site and the Ruth Holmes Whitehead book are especially targeted for children and young people. Many of the other resources are for adults and serious researchers.

Wallace, Birgitta Linderoth, "Vinland 1000—A European Outpost in North America," in *Europe Around the Year 1000*, Przemysław Urbańczyk, editor, and "L'Anse aux Meadows and Vinland: An Abandoned Experiment," in *Contact, Continuity, and Collapse: the Norse Colonization of the North Atlantic*, James H. Barrett, editor.

Whitehead, Ruth Holmes, and McGee, Harold, *The Micmac: How Their Ancestors Lived Five Hundred Years Ago*, Nimbus Publishing Limited, Halifax, N.S., © 1983.

Thanks to Parks Canada and the many individuals whose photographs helped me write this book: H. Beardsley, R. Ferguson, T. Lackey, C. Lindsay, B. Schonback, J. Steeves, and B. Wallace. Thanks also to the Geological Survey of Canada for their air photo.

Construction of house at L'Anse aux Meadows shown in illustration on page 86 is based on a photo by T. Lackey.

Viking Quest Series

Raiders from the Sea
In one harrowing day, Viking raiders capture Bree and her brother Devin and take them from their home in Ireland. After the young Viking leader Mikkel sets Devin free on the Irish coast, Bree and Devin embark on separate journeys to courage.
ISBN: 0-8024-3112-7
ISBN-13: 978-0-8024-3112-7

Mystery of the Silver Coins
Bree finds herself in a physical and spiritual battle for survival in the homeland of her Viking captors. Bree must face her unwillingness to forgive the Vikings, and Mikkel, the Viking leader who captured Bree, begins to wonder: Is the God of these Irish Christians really more powerful than our own Viking gods?
ISBN: 0-8024-3113-5
ISBN-13: 978-0-8024-3113-4

The Invisible Friend

Bree arrives in Norway and is sent to work as a slave for the family of Mikkel, her young Viking captor. She struggles to adjust to the life of a slave, feeling worthless and disrespected, and asking God why He wants her in Norway. As God answers her prayers, Bree faces an important question: No matter who we are or where we live, what does it mean to be truly free?

ISBN: 0-8024-3114-3
ISBN-13: 978-0-8024-3114-1

Heart of Courage

In exchange for Bree's freedom, Devin and Bree have agreed to make one voyage on Mikkel's new Viking ship, Conquest. With explorer Leif Erikson they travel from Norway to Iceland, then to Greenland and beyond, encountering the dangers of the northern waters and an unknown enemy within the ship's crew.

ISBN: 0-8024-3115-1
ISBN-13: 978-08024-3115-8